PERIL ON PROVIDENCE ISLAND

BAKER FAMILY ADVENTURES

PERIL ON PROVIDENCE ISLAND

BY C. R. HEDGCOCK

The Vision Forum, Inc.
4719 Blanco Rd., San Antonio, TX 78212
www.visionforum.com

ISBN   978-1-934554-73-9

Scripture quotations are taken from the King James Version.

Cover Design and Typography by Justin Turley

Printed in the United States of America

"Learn to do good;

Seek justice,

Rebuke the oppressor,

Defend the fatherless,

Plead for the widow."

Isaiah 1:17 [emphases added]

TABLE OF CONTENTS

ACKNOWLEDGMENTS

"Oh, give thanks to the Lord, for He is good! For His mercy endures forever."
–I Chronicles 16:34

To my Heavenly Father I offer thanks and praise for the way He orchestrated things in His Providence to make this book a reality! He opened doors of opportunity beyond my expectations and His grace was there in my every need.

Dad and Mom, your continued support, guidance, and prayers over these months have been invaluable. Thank you also for your exciting ideas to add to the book and all the sacrifices you made to help me focus!

Nicki and Christie, your input and perspectives as older sisters with children of your own are much appreciated. I am very grateful for your suggestions and enthusiasm for the project. To my brother Jonathan, thank you for your feedback and excitement as the story unfolded. I am greatly blessed to have you three as my siblings!

Mr. Josh Lamprecht, thank you for going through the book and offering experienced and practical suggestions for its improvement.

My thanks also go to the many kind people who took an interest in the project, with their encouraging words and inquiries of, "So, how is the book coming on?" Your encouragement and support has been a blessing indeed.

To all who read this story, may you be blessed, challenged, and encouraged, just as I was in writing it. My prayer over these months has been, and still is, that the Lord would use this book for His glory and your edification.

Soli Deo Gloria!
C. R. Hedgcock

INTRODUCTION

Enormous waves swirled around the ship as she rose and fell wildly in the inky blackness. The wind howled ferociously, blasting sea spray onto the deck and into the face of the man at the helm. He quickly wiped his eyes with his wet sleeve and set his face determinedly against the wind, his eyebrows low and his mouth grim. His breath came fast and deep as he locked his eyes straight ahead, trying to ignore the creaking of the ship.

Then, without warning, a sickening, scraping sound was heard over the din of the storm, and the entire ship shuddered violently.

"We've hit a reef!" one of the crewmen cried, his voice high-pitched in fear.

A well-dressed man rushed up from below the deck and strode to the helm. "Mr. Gimsby!" he roared, trying to be heard over the noise.

"We've run aground, Sir!"

"Can you turn her off the rocks at the next large wave and get her to shore?"

"No, Sir! I fear the damage to her hull is too great. She would sink well before we reach the coast. Since the lifeboats are gone, our only hope is to be rescued."

The well-dressed man strained his eyes as he looked in the direction of the distant shore.

"I'm sure there will be lookouts on a night like this," Mr. Gimsby shouted.

"Nobody will take the risk of rescuing us before day breaks and the sea calms," the other man replied. "We'll have pirates upon us before then, especially with the cargo we're carrying."

A particularly large wave lifted the ship up and cast her further onto the reef, making her sway unsteadily with a horrible, scraping sound. Most of the men on deck were knocked off their feet and found themselves sprawling in icy seawater as it poured over the sides of the ship and ran off again. They struggled to their feet, thoroughly drenched.

"Lord, have mercy!" one of them cried.

"Yes," the well-dressed man muttered, raising his eyes to the skies. "Lord, have mercy."

CHAPTER 1

"Abby! Abby! We're landing," Andy whispered urgently, nudging her shoulder.

Twelve-year-old Abby Baker opened her eyes drowsily and looked around. The hum and background ambiance inside the airplane was the same as before, and the lights were coming on.

"Look," Andy said, pointing out the window.

Abby followed her twin brother's gaze. As the plane came gradually lower, glimpses of London Heathrow Airport came into view in the cold, gray light. A shiver of excitement went up Abby's spine. She and her family would be on English soil in mere minutes. They had been planning the trip for months. They would see their grandparents again and celebrate their grandfather's eightieth birthday in a few days, and Abby was sure they'd all have a wonderful time exploring the English countryside together.

She glanced between the seats in front of her to see her oldest brother, Phil, looking out the window in rapt attention.

The plane circled a few times before preparing to land. It came down lower and lower, and finally landed on the runway with a little jolt. There was a whooshing sound as the air brakes engaged, and the passengers felt themselves being pushed against their seat-belts as the plane slowed down.

Once the Bakers had fetched their luggage and gone through customs, they headed for the car-hire booth in the airport.

"Hello, I reserved a car over the Internet," Mr. Baker said in his American accent as he handed a sheet of paper to the immaculately groomed lady behind the desk. She glanced at the sheet, started typing on her computer, and then pulled out some paperwork.

"I'm tired," Tom moaned miserably, leaning against his mother. At five years old, he was the youngest member of the Baker family and the only one who hadn't flown before.

"I know, dear," Mrs. Baker said soothingly, running her hand gently through his hair. "Once we've got our car, you can sleep on the way to Granny's house."

Finally, the lady behind the desk handed Mr. Baker the car keys and said, "Please hold on a moment while I fetch your SatNav."

Andy looked up at his father with a frown. "What's a SatNav?"

"It's the abbreviation for a Satellite Navigation device," Mr. Baker answered. "I'm renting one because using a map on these roads can be nightmarish."

The lady returned with the device and then gave directions to the car park.

The Bakers soon found the large car they were hiring. They packed the trunk, admired the leather seats, and discovered the functions of various buttons while Mr. Baker put an address into the SatNav.

Phil gave a low whistle once it was finished mapping a route. "It's forty-five miles to Grandfather's house. Do you think you'll manage to drive all that way on the wrong side of the road?"

Mr. Baker chuckled. "I'll be fine. I've done it a few times before, so it shouldn't be a difficult adjustment to make."

After getting out of the maze of airport parking areas, Mr. Baker let the SatNav direct him onto the motorway heading north.

The cloud cover had disappeared, and the morning sun shone in the clear sky, casting a golden glow on the scenery. Rolling hills of rich, green grass and trees were on either side of the motorway. Bathed in the morning mist and soft golden light, the view was breathtaking.

"It's green, green, green, as far as your eye can see!" Abby commented in awe.

"I know," Phil nodded. "It's amazing that even the highway ride is pleasant."

"Wow, look over there!" Andy suddenly pointed. "There are sheep on that hillside!"

"Where?" Tom cried.

"There, on that hill on the left, just next to the road."

"Oh look, there are young lambs too," Mrs. Baker added. "Aren't they cute?"

"Imagine keeping your flock of sheep and lambs in a hillside field right next to the highway!" Phil said.

The drive on the motorway was a rather long one, but the twins and Phil were amazed at how pretty England was. At first, all of the Bakers were eager to look out the windows and see the countryside, but after a while, tiredness overtook Mrs. Baker and Tom, and they fell asleep.

"Buckinghamshire," Phil said under his breath, reading the sign they were about to pass.

"Is this where Buckingham Palace is?" Andy asked softly.

"No," Mr. Baker shook his head. "That's in London."

The scenery changed as they drove through Buckinghamshire, past business buildings, more grass and shrubs, and even a forest. When the scene was clear of trees again, Mr. Baker said, "Watch out for this bridge coming up. Try to see what's written on it in spray paint."

"Oh yes, I remember this bridge," Phil smiled.

The twins looked hard as they approached the dark brick bridge.

"Give," Andy said.

"Peas?" Abby read uncertainly.

"A chance," they read together.

"Give peas a chance?" Abby frowned. "Does it really say that?"

Mr. Baker and Phil nodded and laughed, and the twins joined in, though quite incredulously.

"I can't believe somebody would write 'Give peas a chance' on a bridge," Abby said.

"Neither can I," Andy chuckled. "How did the graffiti artist get up there in the first place?"

"I have no idea," Phil replied, shaking his head.

After driving beside open fields, the Bakers passed a sign with the name "Hertfordshire" on it.

Abby leaned her head back and gazed out the window. Her eyelids felt heavy, as though she had kept them open as long as she could. Without meaning to, she soon drifted off to sleep.

The sound of Tom's voice awakened Abby some time later. When she looked up at the SatNav screen, she realized they were only a few miles from their grandparents' house.

They had left the motorway and were driving through a small town. Then they turned onto a tarred, country lane which dipped between two earthen walls, meaning the forest floor was at eye level. The tree canopy closed overhead, making a green tunnel that dimmed the sunlight.

"I forgot how scenic this is!" Mrs. Baker exclaimed.

"Me too," Mr. Baker agreed. He was driving slowly and cautiously around the numerous blind bends.

"Look, there's a squirrel!" Abby pointed as a furry animal scampered across the road ahead.

"Aw, he's cute!" Tom cried.

"I think that's a black squirrel," Mrs. Baker said. "Grandmother told me on the phone that they're a cross between red and gray squirrels, and that they're spreading rapidly."

They watched as the squirrel shot nimbly up a tree. "Hey, Andy," Mr. Baker said, "how would you like to be able to climb a tree that easily?"

The others laughed.

"We're almost there," Mrs. Baker said as they emerged from the forest.

"Wow," Abby breathed. "Imagine living in a place like this!"

Phil and Andy nodded. Wherever they looked, they could only see rich grass, trees, and old cottages with colorful flowerbeds.

"You kids are going to enjoy exploring this area," Mr. Baker said enthusiastically as they reached a fork in the road. To the left was a long avenue of towering oak trees, which led past a collection of cottages. "Turn right," the SatNav directed in a clipped British accent.

The cottages became spaced further apart as the Bakers penetrated deeper into the heart of the English countryside. When their minds were almost full to the brim with country scenes, the SatNav announced, "You have reached your destination."

"We're here!" Abby exclaimed as she peered out the window at the quaintest cottage they had yet passed.

A low, wooden fence and bushes stood in front of the cottage, hiding half of it from view. A rose bush clung to one side of the cottage, and a layer of green moss covered the roof.

The Bakers got out of the car, their excitement overwhelming any remaining fatigue.

"Let's say hello before bringing our luggage in," Mrs. Baker suggested.

They headed towards the cottage, entering the neat garden through the wooden gate.

Mr. Baker rang the bell, and a minute later the door was opened by a dignified-looking, white-haired man, leaning on a walking-stick. Behind him stood a lady with neatly arranged, white hair and gold-rimmed glasses.

"Hello!" Grandfather Wilson exclaimed in a polished accent. "I'm so pleased to see you all!"

Happy greetings filled the air as the Bakers were reunited with Wilson and Janet Drake.

"I do believe," Grandfather said to Tom, "that you were just a baby when we last saw each other. I am Grandfather Wilson," he finished, extending his hand.

"I'm Thomas," he announced, venturing to shake hands. "Pleased to meet you," he laughed, a little embarrassed.

"The pleasure is all mine," Grandfather Wilson laughed.

"Hello Thomas," Granny Janet said in a gentle voice as she gave her youngest grandson a hug.

"Goodness, look how much you've grown, Phil!" Grandfather exclaimed warmly. "The photographs don't do you justice. And you too, Andrew! Why, I have three strapping grandsons!"

"What's strapping?" Tom asked. As one of the grandsons, he thought it was important to know.

"Well," Grandfather answered, "it means healthy, strong, and tall."

"Oh," Tom nodded, standing up straight. He quite agreed with the evaluation.

"Ah, Abby," Grandfather Wilson smiled as she gave him a hug. "You're the one who was forever talking about horses when you were little. Look how you've grown! Well, please all come in and make yourselves comfortable. I'm certain your luggage can wait until you've had some tea and a look around."

"I don't remember you saying anything about a walking-stick, Father," Mrs. Baker said as Grandfather hobbled out of the doorway.

"Oh, it's silly really," Grandfather replied. "I had a minor fall out in the garden a few days ago, and I hurt my foot. Your mother insisted that I use this to lean on."

"Have you been to the doctor?" Mrs. Baker asked.

"Of course not, Alice. You know me," Grandfather chuckled. "It's only a little bruised."

"Would anyone like tea and scones? I baked some earlier this morning," Granny said.

"That sounds wonderful, Mother," Mrs. Baker replied.

"I'm always ready for one of your famous scones," Mr. Baker nodded.

"What are scones?" Tom asked.

Grandfather Wilson faked a shocked expression. "My goodness! You can't be serious, can you? Well, they are . . . hmm," he finished, not sure how to describe them.

"Tom, they're like buns with a crumbly, buttery texture," Mr. Baker explained.

Just then, there was a scratching and whimpering sound at the closed door around the corner.

"Oh! Is that your new dog—the one we saw pictures of?" Andy asked.

"Yes it is," Grandfather Wilson nodded. "He hates being left out of gatherings, but we thought it best, before Tom gets licked to death, to make sure he isn't nervous around dogs."

"He should be fine," Mrs. Baker said. "Mr. and Mrs. Hill have a border collie, and Tom adores her."

"Wonderful!" Grandfather Wilson said.

"Now, Tom," Granny Janet cautioned, "Duke is a little dog, but he gets very excited around new people. He might be rather bouncy because he's happy to see you. If you get scared, we can put him in the garden to let off some energy."

Tom nodded soberly.

Grandfather Wilson opened the door, and a little dog scampered out of the living room, jumping up with joy at the sight of guests. He was delighted when he spotted Tom. He stood up on his back legs and managed to lick the boy's chin, wagging his long, silky tail excitedly.

"He can't believe we have a guest only a little taller than himself!" Grandfather laughed.

Tom didn't seem to know what to do, so Andy scooped up the Cavalier King Charles Spaniel in his arms. The dog turned and started licking his face.

Andy adjusted his position so his face was out of reach. "I'm pleased to meet you too," he said with a laugh. Duke had a long, silken coat, making him cuddly and a pleasure to hold. He had white legs and undersides, and a white stripe on his face. His ears and back were a deep caramel-color.

Phil, Abby, and Tom came over to stroke Duke too.

"Tom, this is Duke," Andy introduced. "Duke, this is Tom. Now you two shake hands."

Tom took Duke's paw and shook it gently, laughing as the dog tried to reach forward and lick his fingers.

"Well," Granny Janet said, turning to Mrs. Baker, "should we get the scones and tea ready? I don't think the children are going to be able to tear themselves away under any other circumstances!"

CHAPTER 2

Mrs. Baker and her mother headed for the kitchen to start getting the food ready. It was a small kitchen, but perfect for the grandparents' needs. The cupboard doors and tabletops were all made of solid oak, and the floor was wooden too.

Abby came in a few minutes later. "Could I help with anything?"

"Yes dear; thank you for asking," Granny Janet answered. "Please put a generous spoonful of clotted cream on the scones that have strawberry jam on them. The cream is just over there."

Abby opened the small, round tub. Deliciously thick, the white cream was under a thin, yellow crust.

"You know, what you're busy doing is rather controversial," Granny Janet remarked as she watched Abby spoon cream onto the jam scones.

"Is it?" Abby asked, pausing with her spoon in mid-air.

Granny Janet nodded. "In Cornwall, cream goes on top of jam on scones. In Devon, jam goes on top of cream on scones!"

"Yes," Mrs. Baker nodded. "Another controversy is over the very name 'scone.' Some people believe it should be pronounced 'skoan,' while others argue that it should be pronounced 'skonn.'

Abby laughed. "I'm sure they taste just as good either way!"

Once the tea and scones were prepared, they were brought to the living room. The room was warm and inviting, though its antique decor was certainly not suited to all tastes.

Upon stepping inside, the first thing to catch Abby's eye was the baby grand piano to the right. Along the walls behind the piano were bookshelves and antique cabinets.

The boys were sitting on the floor in front of the fireplace, playing with Duke, while Mr. Baker and Grandfather talked.

Once they had drunk their tea and savored every bite of their freshly-baked scones, Grandfather announced that he and Granny had small surprises for the children. Granny went out the room and returned with four wrapped presents, which she handed to her eager grandchildren. Phil and Abby were given books; Andy, the least bookish one, was given a small penknife; and Tom was given a fluffy toy dog that looked just like Duke.

Once they had thanked the grandparents, the boys and Mr. Baker headed outside to fetch the luggage while Granny showed Mrs. Baker and Abby the spare rooms.

Abby and Tom had a small but comfortable room to share. Granny then showed the room intended for Mr. and Mrs. Baker. It had a window opening onto a view of fields and rolling hills.

"You have a beautiful cottage, Granny, and everything looks very neat and well-kept," Abby said.

"I'm glad you like it," Granny replied with a smile. "The room Philip and Andrew can share is this way."

She led the way down the corridor, stopping at what looked like a cupboard door. She opened it and felt about the wall for the light-switch. As soon as the light came on, Abby could see a small staircase winding upwards and disappearing around a corner.

"This is really neat!" Abby exclaimed.

"Oh, I used to love this 'secret' passageway!" Mrs. Baker reminisced.

They started climbing up the spiral, wooden staircase, their shoes clattering and the stairs creaking as they went. When they finally reached the top, they were on a wooden landing, faced with a door ahead and a door to the right.

Granny opened the left door and switched on the light. Mrs. Baker and Abby followed her into a medium-sized room in the attic. Its roof slanted steeply towards the left.

On the far side of the room was a desk on which stood an old typewriter. Above the desk was a round window, looking onto a willow tree at the side of the garden.

"The boys will love staying in here," Mrs. Baker said.

"Good. There are two spare mattresses which they can use, but they were too heavy for me to move," Granny continued.

They went back downstairs and explained to Mr. Baker and the boys where to put all the luggage, and Abby offered to show them the rooms.

They spent the next hour or so unpacking luggage and setting up the boys' beds.

"Could we go for a walk?" Andy asked once that was all done. "I'd like to explore this area."

"I was hoping to get some rest," Mrs. Baker answered, looking at the other adults. "I'm really tired after all the stress of traveling."

Mr. Baker nodded. "I am too, especially after all that concentration driving from the airport."

"I can't come with you, Andy, I'm afraid," Grandfather said. "Not with my sore foot."

"I'm rather tired myself. Why don't you go and look around by yourselves?" Granny asked. "You could take Duke with you; he'd be glad of a walk."

Andy looked excitedly at his parents. "Could we?"

"I'm sure it's safe enough in this area," Mrs. Baker said.

Mr. Baker nodded. "If Phil and Duke go with you, I don't mind. Just don't get lost, and be back before dark."

"Yes, Father! Yahoo!" Andy cheered.

"And remember to wear your coats!" Mrs. Baker called over her shoulder. "The air is quite a bit colder here than at home."

Phil, the twins, and Tom dressed warmly and then clipped Duke's lead onto his collar. The dog guessed they were taking him for a walk, and he gave a bark of excitement.

"Andy, have you got your camera?" Phil asked.

"Yep, I've got it!" he said, pulling the strap around his neck.

Andy seemed to have a photographer's eye, and his parents were encouraging him to develop it through practice.

The siblings stepped into the front garden and walked out the wooden gate.

"Which direction should we take?" Andy asked. "If we go right, we'll be going the way we came in the car. I think we should go left, and see what we find that way."

"That sounds good to me," Phil agreed.

They walked along the grass verge beside the road. Duke was enjoying himself immensely, alternately sniffing the air and burying his nose in the grass. Then, he suddenly started barking madly and strained at his lead in his effort to get to a nearby tree.

"Oh look," Phil pointed upwards. "There's a squirrel up there. That must be what he's after."

They managed to coax Duke away from the tree, continuing once more in single file beside the country lane.

They had walked for about ten minutes, admiring and photographing the green fields and farm country, when they heard a "clippety-clop, clippety-clop" behind them and turned around to see a girl on horseback riding up the road.

"Oh," Abby said. "Riding around here must be a lot of fun."

"Yes," Phil nodded. "It could be dangerous, though. Just think of combining horses with cars and blind bends."

"Hmm," Andy agreed, "I would want open space to ride freely in."

They stopped walking and watched as the girl approached. Andy kept a close eye on Duke, but the dog didn't seem perturbed in the least. He sat down, his tail wagging gently.

"That's a beautiful horse," Abby called to the girl, admiring the dark bay's glossy coat.

"Thanks," the girl replied.

"Is he yours?"

The girl nodded.

"Is it safe to ride around here?" Phil asked.

"Yes. Drivers know to expect horse-riders," the girl answered, pulling the reins gently to draw her horse to a stop. "The roads can get busy in the evenings, though."

"Do you have to stay on the road all the time?" Andy inquired.

"No. There are a couple of bridleways through open fields, and even through the forest." She paused, and then asked, "You're from America, aren't you?"

Abby nodded. "Did our accents give us away?"

"I'm afraid so," the girl laughed. She had shoulder-length, straight hair that she wore loose under her riding cap. She looked about sixteen, with an unfortunate lack of modest clothes.

"We're staying with our grandparents, who live here," Abby continued. "Do you know Wilson and Janet Drake?"

The girl raised her eyebrows. "Yes, they live in the cottage next to my grandmother's."

"Really?" Abby asked. "Well, that's amazing." Then she shook her head. "I'm sorry. I'm forgetting my manners. My name is Abigail, this is my twin brother Andrew, my older brother Philip, and my younger brother Tom."

"Hiya," the girl greeted. "My name is Julie."

"Pleased to meet you," Abby answered. "Do you live nearby?"

"I live on Bracken Estate. It's very close," Julie said, shortening her reins.

"Enjoy your ride," Abby finished. "Bye."

"Cheers," Julie replied as she nudged the horse with her heels and resumed her ride.

After exploring the countryside for a good half hour, Phil looked at his watch. "You know," he said, "I think we should start heading home."

"I'm tired," Tom said. "Please can you carry me, Phil?"

Realizing how tired his little brother was, Phil agreed. He squatted down so Tom could climb onto his back, and then stood up and began walking in the other direction.

"We'll be able to catch up on our sleep tonight," he commented cheerily. "English time is about six hours ahead of our time at home. So if we go to bed at ten o'clock here, it's only four in the afternoon there."

"Wow. That is an early night," Abby smiled.

"But," Andy grinned, "if we wake up at eight o'clock tomorrow morning, it'll be two o'clock in the morning at home."

"Even so, Andy," Phil replied, "in your scenario we get a full ten hours' sleep."

Phil and the twins trudged back to the cottage and arrived just before dusk. Duke kept up with them the whole way, trotting on his short legs.

"You're just in time," Mr. Baker welcomed as his four children stepped out of the cool air and into the warm cottage. A delicious smell was wafting from the kitchen. "Granny asks you to please take off your shoes and put them on the rack so the carpets stay clean."

They followed their father into the living room. Duke curled up in front of the crackling logs in the fireplace and closed his eyes.

"Oh good," Grandfather Wilson commented with a smile. "It looks like you've tired Duke out for me."

"He was a very good dog," Andy reported, "except when he spotted a squirrel up in a tree."

"Oh, we should have warned you!" Grandfather chuckled. "That dog is mad about squirrels!"

"We saw a girl riding a horse," Tom said from his comfortable spot on the couch next to his parents. Even though he was tired, he didn't want to pass up the opportunity to be in a conversation.

"Yes," Abby nodded. "Her name is Julie, and she's the neighbor's granddaughter."

"Yes, we know her," Grandfather Wilson said.

"She loves horses and rides frequently in this area," Granny Janet added. "Her parents are managers of Bracken Hall, so they've got a house on the estate."

"Wow," Mrs. Baker raised her eyebrows.

Grandfather Wilson nodded. "There's a public footpath through the estate. You should take a walk through it."

"I'd love to do that," Mrs. Baker replied. "I've always thought it one of the most beautiful places in Hertfordshire."

"Another thing that would be good to do," Granny Janet said in her quiet way, "is go and visit Marge, Julie's grandmother. I know she would be most appreciative of the company."

Just then, in that moment of silence, Andy's stomach growled. Duke raised his head inquisitively with his ears perked up.

Everybody burst into laughter, and Grandfather Wilson turned to Granny Janet and said, "I think that's a cue, my dear!"

Still chuckling, Granny Janet stood up, and she, Mrs. Baker, and Abby headed to the kitchen to dish up supper.

CHAPTER 3

Phil seemed to be right about catching up on sleep, because even though the Bakers were tired when they woke up the next morning, their weariness wore off after a hearty English breakfast.

"Good morning, boys," Granny Janet smiled as Phil and Andy, the last to arrive, came into the living room.

"Good morning," they greeted.

"Did you sleep well?" Mrs. Baker asked.

"Yes, thank you," Phil answered.

Andy nodded. "Very well, thank you. I slept so well, in fact, that I don't think I even heard Phil snore."

"I do not *snore*!" Phil replied in mock horror.

"I heard you," Tom joked.

"Are you sure you weren't hearing *yourself*, Tom?" Abby asked with a grin.

"Oh, so *that's* who it was!" Mr. Baker laughed.

Tom's cheeks flushed pink. "No, no, it wasn't me!"

"All right, Tom, we'll believe that it wasn't you," Grandfather Wilson chuckled. "As for you two," he continued, looking at Phil and Andy, "I hope you don't mind that we've started breakfast already. When it comes to Granny's famous English breakfasts, leaving food to get cold is almost a crime."

"I kept yours in the oven, so it should still be hot," Granny Janet said. "Your orange juice is here, and you can make yourselves coffee if you want."

"Thank you, Granny!" they responded before heading to the kitchen. Inside the oven they found two plates laden with food—scrambled eggs, hash browns, fried tomatoes, mushrooms, baked beans, and toast.

"Wow!" Andy said. "It's certainly a break-*feast*!"

When they came back to the table and started eating their scrumptious breakfast, the adults were discussing what to do that day.

"We're scheduled to go to Bracken Hall today," Grandfather Wilson said.

"Are you?" Abby asked curiously.

"Yes," Grandfather smiled, rubbing his hands together. "Granny and I have to decide what we want on the menu for my birthday party."

"Will you need a third opinion?" Andy asked jokingly. "I've got good taste."

The others laughed at that.

"Maybe we can walk through the grounds while you're busy," Mr. Baker said to the grandparents.

"Yes. We could visit Marge this afternoon," Mrs. Baker added, having a sip of coffee.

Everybody agreed that was a good idea, and Granny Janet offered to phone Marge to ask if they could pop over.

****

Later that morning, Phil and Mr. Baker helped Grandfather Wilson to the passenger seat of his car, a beige Mercedes-Benz. Granny Janet was going to drive, as she wasn't sure how well Grandfather Wilson could do it with a sore foot.

The Bakers climbed into their car, and Mr. Baker followed the beige Mercedes to Bracken Hall. They drove on several quiet lanes before taking a left at a fork where they joined a busy road.

"Ah," Mrs. Baker muttered. "They're taking us the impressive way. We'll pass Bracken Hall as we drive and get a spectacular view of it."

They drove a while longer, with forest on their left.

"Okay, now keep your eyes peeled," Mrs. Baker instructed.

Granny Janet slowed down ahead of them, warning of the clearing in the forest to the left. There, as they passed the clearing, was a view so beautiful that even though it lasted only a few seconds, Abby was able to remember it well.

A tall, iron gate close to the road was the first thing she saw. Stretching beyond it for a long distance was a green lawn framed by hedges. Far away was a grand house perched majestically on a hill.

"*That*," Mrs. Baker paused, "is Bracken Hall."

"Wow," Abby breathed, pulling her eyes away from the window as the house disappeared behind the forest again. "It's beautiful."

They turned off the busy road and arrived at set of open gates. They drove down an avenue of trees, and then approached Bracken Hall in all its glory.

A parking area was on one side of the house, and the Drakes and Bakers pulled up there. Together they strolled to the front of the house.

A calm lake stood at the base of the hill, reflecting the trees along its edge. In the distance stood a stone bridge.

"Well," Mr. Baker said to the grandparents, "shall we walk a little before you go to the restaurant?"

They headed toward the bridge, with Mr. Baker and Phil helping Grandfather Wilson along. After a pleasant time at the bridge, they all headed back to Bracken Hall. Grandfather was helped up the steps, with the rest of the group walking on eagerly.

Abby stepped inside to find herself in a huge entrance hall. The carpet was thick and deep red in color, and a chandelier hung from the ceiling. Straight ahead was an enormous staircase with gold railings.

She drew in her breath sharply, and Andy started snapping away with his camera.

They started going up the stairs, trying to absorb the splendor of the place. At the top of the staircase was the portrait of a nobleman standing proudly beside a fiery red steed.

"That's Lord Bracken," Mrs. Baker said, pointing to a gold plaque beneath the portrait. "This used to be his estate. The heir who owned it two generations ago turned it into a hotel and golf club."

"Wow," Abby breathed, leaning forward to read the plaque. "'Lord George Bracken beside his favorite hunter, Conqueror.' Well, he had an amazing horse."

"Oh! Look there," Andy said, pointing to a brown and white animal in the background. "Now that's amazing!"

"It's Duke!" Tom gasped.

Behind Lord Bracken, beside a cluster of trees, stood a King Charles Spaniel looking upwards.

"Goodness!" Abby laughed, standing on tiptoes for a closer look at the painting. "I do believe he's staring at a squirrel."

The staircase split into two further staircases, one going left and the other going right. As they ascended the left one, they got an eye-level view of the great chandelier, and Andy took the opportunity to capture it on camera.

At the top of the stairs, through a doorway, was an enormous room with lots of windows revealing the spectacular countryside.

"Welcome to the Bracken Hall restaurant," Grandfather Wilson said.

"Oh, I remember this place," Mrs. Baker sighed, fond memories flooding back to her.

Classical music was playing in the background, complementing the 'clink' of fine china and the tinkling of teaspoons caused by diners.

Grandfather Wilson and Granny Janet sat down at one of the tables beside a window, and once they were settled, the Bakers went outside again and began walking back towards the bridge.

They entered the forest on the other side of the lake, enjoying the fresh air and greenery. The footpath narrowed, and the Bakers fell into single file to avoid the thorny plants on either side of the path.

Just then Andy cried out and held up his hand in surprise.

"What happened?" Mr. Baker asked.

"I don't know," Andy replied. "I was walking and something suddenly stung my fingers, over here."

Mrs. Baker took his hand to have a closer look. "You're getting welts. You must have brushed your fingers against this plant."

"I might have," Andy nodded.

"Well, that's a stinging nettle. If you look carefully, you can see tiny, stinging hairs on the surface of the leaves and stem."

"Is the plant dangerous?" Abby asked curiously.

"Oh no," Mrs. Baker answered, giving Andy his hand back. "You'll be fine, Andy."

"Are your fingers really sore?" Abby asked, examining them.

"They're stingy, but not too bad," Andy answered. "I think the suddenness was what got the better of me."

They walked through the forest until they came to a gurgling stream. Several fallen logs lay on the ground, and the Bakers used them as benches, stopping for a little rest until Mr. Baker said it was time to head back.

When they got to Bracken Hall again, it was approaching lunchtime. They all went back to the restaurant to fetch Grandfather and Granny, who had decided what to put on the birthday menu and were just finishing their cups of tea.

They climbed into their cars and drove down the avenue of trees towards the iron gate. When they were still some distance away, however, it started swinging shut.

Granny Janet pulled up in front of the gate, hoping it would open again. After waiting for almost a minute, however, it didn't.

"That's strange!" Mr. Baker said. "It can't be closing time yet."

"No," Mrs. Baker shook her head. "Maybe we should go back to the Hall and ask somebody to open the gate for us."

"Oh look!" Phil exclaimed, looking out the rear window. "There's somebody coming from the Hall."

Abby turned to see a strong man in uniform jogging towards them. As he came close, he slowed to a cautious walk, finally stopping at Mr. Baker's open window.

"I'm afraid you can't leave, Sir," the man said in a polished accent.

"Why not?" Mr. Baker frowned.

"Something has gone missing, and nobody is allowed to leave the Estate until the police have had the opportunity to investigate. I must ask you to return to Bracken Hall."

Abby's jaw slackened in surprise at the news.

"I see," Mr. Baker managed. "Do you have any idea how long the police will take to come? We're on vacation here and have made plans for today."

"My apologies, sir. I can't be sure how long the investigation will take, but I know the police will be here shortly."

As the man went to explain the situation to the grandparents, Mr. Baker carefully turned the car around and drove back to Bracken Hall.

"I wonder what's missing!" Abby exclaimed, her imagination running wild. "Maybe some priceless jewels have been stolen!"

"I doubt that," Phil laughed. "Probably it's something ordinary."

"Imagine if the portrait of Lord Bracken had disappeared," Andy suggested. "Or the huge chandelier."

They all walked to the front entrance again and went up the front stairs. Two uniformed men stood on either side of the door.

"May we search your bags?" one of them asked.

Mrs. Baker gave her handbag to be searched, and Granny Janet did the same. Abby removed the bag that was slung over her shoulder and handed it to one of the guards, who looked in it quickly.

The Bakers then stepped inside Bracken Hall to await the investigation of the police. The front hall was full of people. It seemed everybody from the hotel and restaurant had been instructed to gather there.

The police arrived a few minutes later and were very organized in their investigation. From what Abby could understand, some policemen were searching outside, while some of them went upstairs. Some stayed in the entrance hall, and one of them asked for the crowd's attention.

"I extend my apologies for any inconvenience this investigation may cause you. Something has gone missing from Bracken Hall," he said. "If you have seen or heard any suspicious behavior, please let me or one of my colleagues know all the details. Thank you."

Then the policemen in the entrance hall started talking to people, asking questions and taking notes. One of them came to the group of Bakers.

"Good day, ladies and gentlemen. May I ask if you've seen any suspicious behavior in your time here today? For example, anybody sneaking around?"

Mr. Baker thought carefully and then shook his head. The others also replied in the negative.

"All right. May I have your names then, please?" The man scribbled down their names using his clipboard. "Thank you," he said before moving on to the next group of people.

They waited for another ten minutes, and then policemen and a few members of Bracken Hall staff began coming down the grand staircase. Abby watched as they nodded and exchanged words with the other policemen, and then the same man as before made another announcement.

"Your attention, please! Thank you. Our investigation is complete, and we would like to thank you for your patience and helpful attitude. Once the manager, Mr. Richards, has said a few words, you have our permission to leave."

All eyes moved from the policeman to the tall man standing on the stairs as he began to speak. "On behalf of all the Bracken Hall staff, I would like to extend my sincerest apologies for any inconvenience caused to you. To make up for it, I am offering all of you free drinks from the restaurant. Thank you for your cooperation."

"Hmm," Mrs. Baker muttered as the man finished speaking. "Should we take up his offer and sample the restaurant food at the same time?"

Mr. Baker glanced at his watch. "Well, it is lunchtime, and to be honest, I'm starving!"

"It's a very fine restaurant," Grandfather Wilson said.

"It has a Michelin star," Granny Janet added.

"All right, then," Mr. Baker said. "Maybe this delay has turned out to be a blessing in disguise."

CHAPTER 4

Later that day, after a delicious meal at the Bracken Hall restaurant, the Bakers pulled up outside the grandparents' house. Then they walked down the lane to Marge's cottage. It was rather plain and the garden overgrown, but there was a strong sense of history about it.

"Now children, remember what we told you," Mr. Baker instructed, looking particularly at Tom. "Mrs. Fielding might forget things or use the wrong words, but we must still be polite."

In the car, Mr. and Mrs. Baker had explained what they'd heard about Marge from Grandfather and Granny. Marge had an illness called Alzheimer's Disease which made her forgetful and often confused. The children knew that the lady needed them to be especially kind and patient.

Grandfather Wilson rang the doorbell, and some minutes later the front door was opened by a very elderly lady. Her face was crinkled and worn by years of time, and her lips were barely pink. She was of average size and height, with sunken cheeks, an expressive mouth, and watery, blue eyes behind large glasses. Her short, curly hair was snowy white.

"Hello, Marge," Granny Janet greeted calmly. "It's good to see you."

"Oh, hello," the lady replied in a wavering voice. Tom began to wonder if voices could run out after a long time.

"Good afternoon!" Grandfather Wilson greeted.

"This is my daughter and her family," Granny Janet continued. "Here is my daughter Alice –"

"Hello," Mrs. Baker smiled.

"My son-in-law Charles," Granny Janet continued.

"Pleased to meet you," he said.

"And my grandchildren," Granny Janet said. "Philip, Andrew, Abigail, and Thomas."

"What lovely names," Marge replied in her old voice. "It is very kind of you to visit. My name is Margaret Fielding, but people call me 'Old Marge.'" She chuckled quietly, and then said, "Please, do come in."

They filed into her cottage, which looked even older than she did. The elderly lady hobbled into the living room, heading for a rocking chair beside the fireplace.

"Please, take a seat and make yourselves comfortable. It's not often that I have company," she said, sinking down into the soft cushions on the rocking chair. "You don't mind if I knit, do you?"

"Not at all," Granny Janet answered.

She reached down and pulled something fluffy and purple from the basket at her side. Two knitting needles appeared as she slowly unfolded the fluffy bundle, and then a ball of wool tumbled out and landed on the floor. Old Marge started weaving the knitting needles back and forth, catching loops of wool with surprising speed and dexterity.

"You have a lovely cottage," Mrs. Baker commented as she looked around the room and out the window.

"Thank you," Old Marge said with a smile. "It's small, but full of old memories."

"We went to Bracken Hall this morning, Marge," Granny Janet said, gently changing the subject.

"Did you?" Old Marge asked, somewhat blankly.

"Yes," Grandfather Wilson nodded. "You know, that great house and estate your daughter Sue and son-in-law Peter look after."

"It's beautiful," Mrs. Baker said. "We had a lovely walk over the bridge and through the forest. Looking after such an enormous place must be a difficult job."

"Yes," Old Marge said. "You're not from around here, are you?"

"No," Mrs. Baker shook her head. "We arrived yesterday from the United States. We've come here for my father's eightieth birthday."

"I trust you're enjoying your time here in England." Marge sighed. "Eighty years old sounds rather young."

"Really?" Tom blurted, only thinking the better of it when his mother looked emphatically at him. "I'm sorry," he said. "Was that rude?"

The grandparents and Old Marge chuckled heartily.

"You must have some amazing stories to tell," Andy said. "Do you remember anything about the Second World War?"

Old Marge slowly stopped knitting and looked up, her eyes taking on a thoughtful look. "I do," she said slowly. "I was just sixteen years old when it started. My dear father and my brother Arthur went off to war, and I didn't know when I would see them again for the next few years. It was very difficult for my mother and me."

"I'm sure it was," Abby said sympathetically.

"I have some photographs of us back then," Old Marge said, setting her knitting down, getting up, and pulling an album from the bookshelf against the wall. She handed it to Abby, who opened it out on her lap. Mrs. Baker and Phil leaned over from either side to get a look at the photos too.

"Could you please tell us any of your family history?" Phil asked.

"Well, I can tell you my favorite tale that was passed down in my family. One of my ancestors, Sir Edward Jenkins, was a wealthy merchant who made his fortune by trading on the high seas."

She closed her eyes, her voice dreamy. "Arthur and I loved to hear Father tell the story. My great-great-great-great-great-grandfather was the wealthy merchant. He was carrying a load of something precious when the sea whipped up into a violent storm. Rain poured down in sheets upon the ship's deck, so that none of the crew could see where they were going. All they knew was that they were near the coast of . . . of Southampton. No, of Bristol. That doesn't sound quite right either. Well, the important thing is that they were in an area where fearsome pirates prowled.

"The ship was cast upon some rocks, and the merchant knew he would be stranded until help arrived. He suspected that pirates would be on the scene long before that. So, in order that his personal fortune of gold coins wouldn't be seized, he sealed them in a chest, and threw the chest overboard.

"The sun rose the next morning, and the pirates did come. They engaged in a fierce battle, took the valuable cargo, and made prisoners of all on board." She opened her eyes.

"What happened to the treasure?" Tom asked.

"It was never found."

"What happened to –" Abby began, interrupted by the telephone ringing.

"I'm sorry. Please excuse me," Old Marge said as she slowly raised herself out of her rocking chair and shuffled to the phone.

"Hello?" she answered.

"Quite a swashbuckling tale," Abby whispered softly while waiting for Old Marge to finish the call.

Phil nodded.

"It makes you wonder if the treasure is still at the bottom of the ocean," Andy said.

"I doubt that," Phil whispered. "Probably the merchant came back for it."

Old Marge was talking so loudly into the phone that the others couldn't help overhearing her.

"Thank you, Sue. I would appreciate that. The fridge is almost empty now." There was a pause. "Yes, love, thanks for helping with the bills. You take care of yourself. Yes, yes, I will. I've got some friends over. Janet and her daughter's family. Love you. Bye-bye."

Old Marge shuffled back from the telephone and sank down on her rocking chair again. "I'm sorry about that disturbance; my daughter Sue phoned. What were we busy talking about?"

"I was about to ask what happened to the merchant once he was caught by the pirates," Abby said.

Old Marge frowned, and then at the mention of pirates her brow smoothed. "Oh! Were we talking about *that*? Pirates?" She chuckled. "It was one of dear Arthur's favorite operas. Well, Frederic wasn't *caught* by pirates; he was apprenticed to them by his nurse when he was just a boy. He was finally free to leave, and...."

"Uh, I'm sorry to interrupt, Marge," Grandfather Wilson hesitated, "but we're not talking about the same story."

Old Marge looked from one face to the other.

"Marge," Granny Janet said softly, "we weren't talking about the opera 'The Pirates of Penzance.'"

"Weren't we?" Old Marge frowned. "Then what pirates did you mean?" she asked Abby.

"You were telling us about your ancestor, who threw a treasure chest into the ocean before his ship was captured by *pirates*," Abby said, hoping to refresh Old Marge's memory.

Old Marge thought for a moment. "That does sound vaguely familiar. It was a very exciting story that Arthur liked to hear."

"Can't you remember it?" Andy asked. "You said the merchant's name was Edward, and that his ship was in a storm off the coast of Bristol or Southampton."

"No," Old Marge shook her head. "It wasn't either of those places. It was in Cornwall. Penzance is very likely. That's where the pirates were, of course."

Abby sighed inwardly in disappointment.

"Never mind," Granny Janet said. "Perhaps you'll remember some other time. How have you been doing? You know that if you ever need us, Wilson and I will do all we can to help."

"Thank you, Janet, you are very kind. Well, something has been upsetting me lately. As this area is becoming more and more popular, my bills are increasing outrageously. Well, the truth is, I don't know how much longer I'll be able to keep up with them."

Mr. and Mrs. Baker cast concerned glances at each other.

"What about Sue? Is she able to help you?" Granny Janet asked slowly.

"Well, yes, and she has been helping a lot," Old Marge paused sadly, "but I don't want to be a burden."

"Marge, I'm sure Sue and Peter can cope perfectly well," Grandfather Wilson countered. "Besides, they live very nearby. Bracken Hall is barely a ten minute drive away."

"It's not only that," Old Marge muttered. "Sue thinks I need special care. She wants me to leave my cottage and go to live at a home for senior citizens." Old Marge shook her head. "I don't want to leave. I've always wanted to spend my last days here."

"Couldn't you employ a care-worker?" Grandfather Wilson suggested.

Old Marge shrugged. "I don't know."

"I'm sorry to hear this," Granny Janet said. "I wouldn't mind talking to Sue, if that would help."

The rest of the time at Old Marge's cottage passed pleasantly, with the conversation turning onto topics like wildflowers, edible mushrooms, and musical instruments. Old Marge was very knowledgeable and could impart understanding on a variety of subjects.

The Bakers felt glad they had been able to meet the elderly widow and hopefully bring her joy. At heart though, they felt grieved at the thought of her having to leave her dear cottage.

"Thank you for welcoming us into your home, Marge," Mr. Baker had said as they prepared to leave.

"You're most welcome. Thank you for keeping me company. It was a pleasure to meet you all," Old Marge replied, putting her knitting project back in the basket beside her rocking-chair and rising slowly to her feet.

"Goodbye," the Bakers said, one at a time.

"Goodbye," she replied, following her guests to the door and waving as they walked away. Abby noticed Old Marge watching them until they were out of sight.

"She's a dear lady, isn't she?" Mrs. Baker said.

"Yes, she is," Granny Janet replied.

"I'm glad we were warned about her Alzheimer's," Abby confessed.

Andy nodded in agreement.

"I was sad that she couldn't finish her story," Tom said. "What do you think happened to the man, Father?"

"I'm not sure," Mr. Baker replied, shaking his head. "Maybe the story didn't actually happen. It might be from another opera, novel, or film that Marge confused with reality."

Abby nodded sadly. "You're probably right. I wish daring adventures didn't *only* happen in people's imaginations."

"That's for sure," Andy agreed.

****

A few hours later, the Bakers and grandparents were chatting at the table after savoring Granny Janet's delicious macaroni cheese.

"Mrs. Fielding is very learned," Phil commented, following on from the conversation they had been having.

Granny Janet nodded. "You can always be sure to learn something from her if you have the time to listen."

"Grandfather," Abby said thoughtfully, "what opera did Mrs. Fielding start telling us about?"

"Gilbert and Sullivan's 'The Pirates of Penzance,'" Grandfather Wilson replied. It's a famous opera from the late 1800s about pirates who lurked around the town of Penzance, in Cornwall."

"So Penzance is a real place?" Andy asked curiously.

"Oh yes," Grandfather Wilson answered. "Granny and I have been there a number of times."

"Yes, and we always make a joke about the opera when we're there," Granny Janet laughed. "Cornwall is a beautiful place. If you had more time in England, I would suggest you make a trip there."

Grandfather Wilson nodded. "The weather can be delightful, with pleasant sunshine and cool, sea breezes. There you'll see picturesque towns with cobbled streets fanning out past old shops selling ice cream, rock candy, and famous Cornish pasties. There are sandy beaches and a bright blue ocean, and if you look out to sea, you may spot a lighthouse on a speck of an island."

"Of course, you don't have to go to Penzance," Granny Janet said. "You could go to see St. Michael's Mount. When the tide is in, it's an island. When the tide is out, you can walk there."

"Yes, or the Lizard peninsula," Grandfather Wilson added. "It's the southernmost place in England, and famous for smugglers."

Mrs. Baker laughed. "It's a pity that Cornwall is five hundred miles from here."

"Yes," Granny Janet agreed. "Traveling there would take at least a six-hour drive."

"Well, we came to England to see you and to celebrate Father's birthday," Mrs. Baker said. "Maybe we can visit Cornwall on another trip."

"Yes," Mr. Baker nodded. "We planned to spend the last days of our vacation here as typical tourists. We're going to take a day-trip into London to see the sights, and another day to go to Cambridge, and another day to go to Oxford, and so on."

"I'm sorry to sound like a broken record," Abby said, "but I wish Mrs. Fielding's story *was* true."

Granny Janet smiled sympathetically as she reached forward to pat Abby's hand. "Well dear, what is true is that you're on holiday in England, that you're here with grandparents who love you, and that there's a sticky toffee pudding in the oven."

CHAPTER 5

The next day, the Bakers were kept busy with their preparations for Grandfather Wilson's eightieth birthday party. Because many family members were coming, a suitable venue had been hired. Bracken Hall had been chosen, months before, by Mrs. Baker's older brother Clive.

"So the party tonight is going to be at Bracken Hall?" Abby asked. She had heard the party plans a long time ago, but only then realized what a grand venue had been chosen.

"Yes," Mrs. Baker nodded. "We're hiring the restaurant for the evening."

"Wow," Phil commented. "That'll be memorable. The food is really delicious there."

"Yes," Andy nodded with a grin.

"We're going to decorate the restaurant this evening," Mrs. Baker continued. "Uncle Clive has organized all the decorations, but I've offered our help in putting them up. I think you should all go over those speeches you wrote and memorized."

"Mother, is Uncle Clive bringing a projector?" Phil asked.

"He said there's one at Bracken Hall," Mrs. Baker replied.

The Bakers had planned for their photo slideshow to be projected onto a screen in the restaurant.

The rest of the day was spent in anxious anticipation. There were shirts and dresses to iron, and speeches to rehearse once Grandfather had been persuaded to join Granny in taking a pot of soup to Marge's house.

"We must also make sure she's remembered that the party is tonight," Granny Janet had said.

After lunch, there was time for a walk with Duke and the chance to explore church ruins nearby.

When the Bakers got home, they dressed up, fetched their speeches and DVD slideshow, and drove to Bracken Hall. Granny Janet would drive Grandfather Wilson there later that evening.

Abby tapped her feet in nervous excitement as their car neared Bracken Hall. It looked even grander in the warm light of sunset that reflected off the lake.

One other car was already there—and it was a shiny, black Rolls-Royce.

"Clive's here," Mrs. Baker noted.

They pulled up beside his car, climbed out, and took everything out of the trunk.

Abby's heart thumped with excitement as they walked, much too slowly it seemed, to the front of the house and up the steps. They filed inside the entrance, which was glowing with golden light from the chandelier, and made their way up the stairs to the restaurant. A few people were standing off to one side, and they turned when the Bakers entered.

"Alice!" Uncle Clive exclaimed, striding over to welcome his younger sister and her family. "Hi Charles," he smiled, shaking hands with Mr. Baker enthusiastically. "Phil, Andy, Abby, Tom—it's great to see you all again."

"Hel-*lo*," Aunt Susan greeted, joining the group with a wide smile. Her red lipstick framed a perfect set of teeth. "It's *charming* to see you."

"Hi," Millie said as she arrived from the other side of the room. Her blonde hair was short and straight, as before, but her eye makeup wasn't as dark as the previous summer.

"Hey, Millie!" Abby beamed, stepping forward to give her cousin a hug. "How are you doing?"

"Great," Millie replied. "How are your horses?"

"Oh, they're well thanks. How's Calvin?"

"A dream horse, as always. Together we're learning dressage moves that we'll use in a show later in the year."

"How exciting!" Abby returned.

While the two girls helped with decorations, they filled each other in on the latest events in their lives. Naturally, Millie's news seemed far more interesting to Abby than her own. Millie told Abby that things had been getting difficult for her at school, and how her father had decided to get her a private tutor instead.

"So, I'm going to continue school until the next holidays," Millie finished, "and then the private tutor will come and teach me instead."

"That's wonderful news! I hope you enjoy staying home as much as I do."

"I'm sure I will," Millie nodded. "The tutor is a lady named Mrs. Smith, and she's very kind and patient. We'll get along well."

Time sped by as the girls worked, until Aunt Susan came up to them with a shocked expression on her face. "Mildred!" she gasped. "The guests are arriving any minute now, and you're not even dressed yet!"

She herself looked beautiful. Her blonde hair was styled in an impressive arrangement on her head, and she was wearing a bright red dress. Glancing at the glamorous splendor of Aunt Susan and then at Millie, Abby could almost understand Aunt Susan's anxiety.

"All right," Millie replied. "I'll go now."

Millie returned some time later in a black dress and patent-leather heels.

"Your dress looks very classy," Abby commented.

Millie laughed. "I guess so. I like your dress too - the dark purple suits you."

Phil, Andy, and Tom were standing near the door of the restaurant, looking very smart in their suits. The girls joined them there, ready to welcome the guests when they arrived.

"Mother says I look grown up," Tom said, standing up straight and clasping his hands together. "Do you think so?"

Abby laughed and nodded.

Millie smiled. "Definitely."

The guests starting arriving about five minutes later, and the children did a wonderful job of welcoming and directing them to their tables.

Once all the guests had arrived, including Marge, Julie, and Julie's parents, Uncle Clive stood up and gave an introduction, and Grandfather Wilson said grace. Then it was time for supper, and well-groomed waiters began gliding unobtrusively around tables to take orders.

The tables were round, and the seating arrangements had been carefully pre-arranged. The four Baker siblings were at one table, along with Millie and Julie. That gave them the chance to get to know Julie better and to tell her about homeschooling, which she didn't seem to know much about and found most intriguing.

After the delicious supper, there were touching speeches from many of the guests, and thankfully all the Bakers remembered theirs. Then the slideshow of Grandfather's life was projected onto the wall.

Overall, the celebration was a great success. Grandfather Wilson stood up afterwards and thanked everybody for their thoughtfulness, and more than a few people noticed tears well up in his clear blue eyes.

The waiters again appeared, and started taking dessert orders. There was an assortment of mouth-watering options on the menu, and the most popular ones of the evening were the hot, chocolate fondant with vanilla ice cream, the caramel shortbread surprise, and the Eton mess, a dessert made with strawberries, cream, and pieces of meringue.

When all the planned events were finished, the pleasant hum of conversation filled the air, and some of the children began to get restless, particularly Tom after his sugary dessert.

"I wonder if we could go outside," Andy said. He turned to see through a window, but they were all covered by curtains.

"I'm not sure that's the best idea," Phil replied, glancing at their smart clothes.

"What else *could* we do?" Abby wondered aloud.

"Hmm," Julie muttered. "Excuse me, I just want to ask my dad something." She returned a minute later. "My dad said I could show you around the house, if you'd like."

"A guided tour?" Andy grinned.

Julie nodded. "I do give tours in the holidays sometimes."

"I'd love to see around the house," Abby said excitedly. "Thanks!"

Mr. and Mrs. Baker were surprised by the kind offer, and they happily gave their consent for the children to look around with Julie.

Julie led the Baker siblings and Millie down the grand staircase. "We'll start at the bottom floor and work our way upwards," she explained as they absorbed the magnificence of their surroundings.

"Around this side of the building are the art galleries used by Lord Bracken in the early 1700s," Julie said matter-of-factly as they walked down a spacious passageway.

The floor was wooden, but a long carpet ran down the middle. "We are now entering the first of these galleries, commonly called the 'Landscape Gallery.'"

"Did Lord Bracken collect all these paintings?" Abby asked in awe, looking around at the many paintings adorning the walls of the long room.

Julie nodded. "Yes. He was very fond of art, but also had a very particular taste, which he passed on to his son and heir, George."

"Interesting," Phil commented.

Abby nodded. "I love the paintings he chose. These landscapes are beautiful, and there is such a range of them."

Julie nodded. "Shall we move on to the next gallery?"

They walked to the end of the landscape gallery, where a door led onto another long room. "This is the 'Animal Gallery.' Here we can see the Brackens' love of animals."

"Oh!" Abby gasped. "This is my favorite gallery so far."

"Mine too," Andy said.

"And mine," Tom agreed enthusiastically.

Portraits of dogs, big and small, were the most numerous, with paintings of prancing colts and majestic horses coming in close second.

"Most of these animals were owned by Lord Bracken or his children," Julie said. "Shall we go on? The next gallery contains portraits of Lord Bracken's family and friends. It was his favorite gallery of all."

They went on to the last gallery, which was a room larger and wider than the rest. The roof was high, making the place feel spacious, and at the end of the room stood luxurious armchairs.

"Here are the portraits of Lord Bracken's family members," Julie pointed out. "Here are his parents, his one sister, his wife, and his three children. The rest of the gallery contains other paintings that Lord Bracken particularly liked."

Tom, who was by that time getting bored of admiring the paintings, went on ahead of the others, going down to the bottom of the room and coming back up the other side.

"Whoa!" he exclaimed suddenly. "Look at this ship!"

Phil went over to the other side to see the painting. "I wouldn't like to be on that ship, eh Tom?" he said. "It looks stranded on those rocks."

Tom nodded. "And look at those waves! Swish, swoosh!" he said, with accompanying hand motions.

Phil was about to move on when he chanced to look at the next portrait. "Wait a second," he muttered to himself, looking closer at the plaque beneath it. "This man is named Edward Jenkins. Now why does that name sound familiar?"

Tom shrugged. "I don't know."

"Maybe you want to have a look at this," Phil called to the others. "It's a portrait of a man named Edward Jenkins."

"Really?!" Abby gasped. "Do you remember? Mrs. Fielding said the name of her wealthy ancestor was Edward Jenkins!"

"Could it really be the same person?" Andy asked curiously.

"It probably is," Julie answered, not sounding surprised. "Are you asking if that man is related to my grandmother?"

"Yes," Abby said.

"He is," Julie nodded. "Edward Jenkins was a dear friend of Lord Bracken, who often invited Edward and his family for a holiday here. When Edward retired, Lord Bracken offered him the job of looking after the estate. The job has gone down the generations, all the way to my mum."

"Fascinating," Phil said.

"Maybe you can tell us the end of Edward's story. Mrs. Fielding told us how he was captured by pirates. What happened to him? And what happened to his treasure?" Abby asked.

Julie shook her head. "Oh, so you heard *that* story. Look, it's about pirates and sailing, and would be great in an adventure book. But it's the kind of thing you can't bring yourself to believe. My gran has Alzheimer's, so don't take seriously anything she says."

"The story could be true," Abby persisted.

"He was a merchant, after all," Andy added. "He must have had encounters with pirates."

Julie frowned. "Shipwreck? Buried treasure? You can't be serious."

"Just look at this ship," Phil said, pointing to the painting. "It's stranded on the rocks, just as Mrs. Fielding described. It's also right beside a portrait of Edward Jenkins."

"Surely that means something," Andy added.

Julie shrugged. "I don't want to argue. Let's just continue going around the house."

Julie led the way back through the galleries and up the grand staircase to the side of the house opposite the restaurant.

"This part of the house was used by the Brackens for entertaining family friends, and also for private study and tutelage. Here is the library," she said as she walked through a doorway and into a huge room, its walls lined with bookshelves all the way up to the ceiling.

"Oh!" Abby cried. "It's perfect! Look, there's even a fireplace and comfortable reading chairs around it. This is a dream come true."

Julie laughed. "Well then, go and have a look around."

Abby didn't need any more encouragement. She started wandering around the library, studying the titles of books with fascination. She walked down a side of the room which held the oldest books in glass cabinets—moth-eaten cotton-covers and tattered leather-bounds.

She squinted at the faded words on the binding of one of the books. "Diary of . . . Jane . . . Bracken." She raised her eyebrows. "This cabinet must be full of ancient diaries!" she breathed. "Imagine all the history behind this glass!"

She took a step further and read the next title. "Wow, this is Lord Bracken's diary!" she said, loud enough for the others to hear.

"Really?" Andy asked, coming to see. He looked through the glass at the book Abby pointed to.

Julie came over. "So you've found the diary section."

"This would be a historian's paradise!" Abby replied as she continued reading the titles.

The others lost interest and looked around other places in the library. Eventually Phil came over to say, "Abs, I think we should move on now. The rest of us want to see the state rooms."

"Oh, Phil, look at this," Abby said with shining eyes. She pointed at an old book. "That's a diary belonging to Edward Jenkins."

"Really?" Phil gasped. "That could tell us whether his shipwreck adventure happened or not."

"Just look at the next titles," Abby continued, pointing. "These three are also Edward's diaries."

"Three more?" Phil asked, amazed.

"I wonder which is the right one to look through to find the account of the shipwreck."

"The best way to find out would be to ask Mrs. Fielding the date of Edward's adventure and go from there," Phil replied.

"We could try, but I don't think she even remembers that she told us that story, never mind the details of it."

"Maybe she will," Phil said. "Let's ask her, and then find out from Julie's father if we can sit here and read the diaries."

"Okay," Abby agreed.

CHAPTER 6

Entering the restaurant, Phil and Abby soon found the table Old Marge was sitting at. She didn't seem to be in conversation with anybody, so Phil didn't feel he was being impolite.

"Excuse me, Mrs. Fielding," he said.

"Hello," she replied.

"Mrs. Fielding, when we went to your house, you told us the story of the wealthy merchant Edward Jenkins, your ancestor."

Old Marge only frowned. "I don't know what you're talking about."

Mr. Richards, Julie's father, leaned over to Phil. "She's got Alzheimer's," he said, as though that was sufficient explanation.

"Yes, sir," Phil replied. "Mrs. Fielding told us a story about her ancestor Edward. Julie showed us the library, and my sister found several diaries belonging to him. We thought perhaps he would have written about his adventure if it had really happened. Would we be allowed to sit in the library and read through the diaries?"

Mr. Richards looked uncertain. "I am the manager of the Estate, but Mr. Toole is the trustee until Cyril Bracken comes of age. Did you say there were diaries written by Edward Jenkins in the library?"

"Yes," Phil answered. Abby nodded.

"I'd like to see those," he said, standing up. "Please excuse me," he said to the other people around his table.

He led the way to the library, and then Abby and Phil showed him the cabinet where the diaries were.

"They're right . . . here," Abby finished with a puzzled look. Several books were missing from the shelf, leaving a large gap between the other books. "That's strange," she said. "They were here when we left."

"Yes, they were," Phil agreed.

"Then where have they gone?" Abby wondered aloud.

"Do you mean to say that there are books—diaries—missing from this library?" Mr. Richards asked in a serious voice.

"It appears so," Phil replied soberly.

"Where's Julie?" Mr. Richards asked sternly.

"The last I heard her say is that she was going to lead us to the state rooms," Phil answered.

"You two, come with me." With that, Mr. Richards turned on his heels and strode out of the library. Abby almost had to jog to keep up with him and Phil. They went through a large hallway and into a spacious room. Julie and the others were there.

"Julie," Mr. Richards called, his voice strong and deep. "Julie, what have I told you about leaving people behind?"

"Oh!" she gasped, surprised to see her father. "I didn't notice they weren't with us."

"Did you take any diaries from the library?"

Julie shook her head quickly. "No, I didn't touch them."

Mr. Richards dismissed the thought. "Go fetch Gus, and tell him to call the police. It seems we've had another robbery, this time in the library. The rest of you, come with me."

They filed out of the room and went back to the library. A few minutes later, they were joined by Julie and the burly security guard the Bakers had met on their previous visit to Bracken Hall.

"Look—several books missing, Gus," Mr. Richards said, pointing to the bookshelf.

Gus peered through the glass to inspect the gap between the other old books. "If it was the same person as last time, he won't have left any fingerprints."

"He must have somehow forged a key. Has somebody started checking the surveillance cameras?"

"Yes," Gus nodded. "David's on the job."

"And the police?"

"On their way."

"Mr. Richards, we were here when something went missing yesterday," Phil said. "Was there a thief involved, and was he caught?"

"There was a thief involved," Mr. Richards answered, "but he hasn't been caught—yet."

"What did he take?" Andy asked.

"An old document."

Abby frowned.

"Is there a copy of the document we could see?" Phil asked. "It might give a clue as to why Edward Jenkins' diaries have also been taken."

"I'm sorry, but this investigation is for the police," Mr. Richards replied.

"You could get Detective Mortimer to help you," Tom suggested.

"Yes!" Abby nodded. "We know a British private detective who could solve this mystery for you."

"I would also recommend him," Millie added.

"What did you say his name was?" Mr. Richards asked.

"Detective Mortimer Jones," Phil answered. "He's a professional who helped us with a very tricky scenario. You might have heard of the Great Verton jewelry theft organization."

"The Verton jewelry thieves? Why, that was all over the news!" Mr.

Richards spluttered in amazement. "Were you the kids mixed up in that story? That's extraordinary! Is your Detective Mortimer the one who cracked the case?"

Phil nodded.

"And you say he's British? Gus, get somebody to look up that detective," Mr. Richards instructed. "We need the very best for the job."

The police arrived, and the Bakers, Millie, and Julie had to leave the library after answering a couple of questions. Naturally, they couldn't help very much, but they hoped the police would be able to make progress anyway.

"Julie, didn't your dad mention surveillance cameras?" Millie asked.

"Yes, they're posted all over the place."

"Then surely the thief must be caught on film," Millie continued.

"He is," Julie nodded, "but you can't tell much about him that way. I've seen the video clips from last time, and he was completely dressed in black, even with a balaclava over his face."

"That must look very suspicious," Andy said.

"Yes," Phil agreed. "If anybody saw him walking around like that, they would surely suspect something. Isn't there somebody watching the cameras all the time who could alert the security guards?"

Julie shrugged her shoulders.

"The last burglary happened during the day," Andy pointed out. "Why didn't somebody notify the security guards of suspicious behavior? And why wasn't the thief caught if he was on camera?"

"Look, I don't know," Julie sighed. "All I know is that there were a lot of people around that day, and the thief got mixed up in the crowd. The camera operator could easily have looked away at the precise moment the burglary happened."

"All right, all right," Phil said. "Let's not get too wound up about this. The police are here, and probably Detective Mortimer will be hired soon. Let's go back to the restaurant. Tom looks over-tired and in need of some rest."

When they walked into the restaurant, a surprising scene met their eyes. Old Marge was sprawled on the floor and a group of people were standing around her.

Julie gasped and dashed over to see what had happened, and the Bakers and Millie were right behind her.

"What happened?" Julie asked her mother in concern.

"She stood up without any warning, took a few steps, and lost her balance," Sue Richards answered. "I've already called the ambulance."

"Thank goodness!" Julie breathed, resting her hand over her heart as she saw Old Marge blinking. She was relieved that her grandmother didn't seem to be badly hurt.

"Where's your dad?" Sue Richards asked Julie softly as she neared her daughter.

Julie leaned forward to whisper a reply in her mother's ear. Mrs. Richards' eyes widened, and she looked anxious.

The paramedics rushed into the room, calling for people to move out the way as they wheeled in a stretcher. After doing some quick checks and getting some details from Mrs. Richards, they began to lift Old Marge onto the stretcher.

"We're going to take you to the hospital," one of them explained.

"I'm fine. I'm fine," she insisted.

"Everything will be all right, Mum," Mrs. Richards assured Marge.

"Are you sure this is necessary?" Mr. Baker asked.

"Her blood pressure is higher than average," one of the paramedics answered. "The best place to watch her is at the hospital, where her condition can be closely monitored."

It took a while for things to quiet down again after the paramedics left. The Bakers felt worried that the scenario was a convenient ploy to get Old Marge out of her cottage. Grandfather Wilson and Granny Janet decided to talk to Mrs. Richards.

"Sue," Granny Janet said softly as they approached, "could we talk?"

The three of them went into a quiet corner.

"Sue, when we visited Marge she told me she was worried about losing the cottage and going into a care home," Granny Janet said tactfully.

Sue Richards sighed. "You must try to see things from our perspective too. We work hard here at Bracken Estate, and we're kept busy all the time. Looking after a mother with Alzheimer's is a huge burden, and I feel she's reaching the point where she can't live by herself anymore."

"So you think sending her off to a care home is the answer?" Grandfather Wilson asked.

"Well, yes. With her in a care home, we can have the assurance that she's being looked after properly. That little cottage would bring in a decent amount of rent money, which would cover the care-home bills. So you see, it's a simple solution to the problem."

Granny Janet blinked sadly. "Isn't the cottage hers? Would you be allowed to rent it out?"

"We would be renting it out on her behalf."

"Wouldn't you consider letting her live out her days in the comfort of her own home, and employing a care worker?" Grandfather Wilson suggested.

Sue held up her hand. "Look, we don't have it all figured out yet. I appreciate your concern, but we have to make the decision. Now, please excuse me. It's very important that I find my husband."

The two grandparents went back to their table to find the Baker siblings and Millie in discussion with Mr. and Mrs. Baker.

"Extraordinary!" Mrs. Baker said, shaking her head. She turned to her parents. "Did you hear that there was a burglary in the library tonight?"

"No," Grandfather said, his curiosity piqued.

"Tell the story again, Phil," Mr. Baker said.

"Julie was taking us on a tour of the building, starting downstairs and continuing upstairs into the library. When we were downstairs in the art galleries, Tom found a painting of a ship that had run aground on rocks in a violent storm. Beside that painting was a portrait of *Edward Jenkins*, the wealthy merchant Mrs. Fielding was telling us about! Julie said that he was a good friend of Lord Bracken and often came here on vacation."

"And that's why he got the job of looking after the estate," Abby added quickly. "It's gone down the generations, all the way to Mrs. Richards."

"How interesting!" Grandfather Wilson rumbled, deep in thought.

"Well, we went upstairs to the library where Abby got distracted with the books. When I went to tell her that the others were moving on, she had just discovered diaries belonging to—guess who—*Edward Jenkins*."

"Really?" Granny gasped.

"Yes!" Phil paused as his grandparents marveled at the news. "We decided to come back here and ask Mrs. Fielding if she could remember the date of Edward's shipwreck, and ask Mr. Richards if we could look through the diaries to see if there are any accounts of it."

"And?" Grandfather prodded.

"Mrs. Fielding didn't know what we were talking about, and Mr. Richards wanted to see the diaries we had mentioned. Abby and I went to the library with him, and showed him the cabinet where Edward's diaries had been in— but they were gone."

Granny gasped again.

"Gone?" Grandfather muttered. "What do you mean?"

"There was no sign of them at all," Phil answered.

"The police are busy investigating now. I think the diaries must have been stolen," Abby added.

"They must have been taken while you were here in the restaurant," Grandfather Wilson said in disbelief. "That might mean," he paused, "that somebody was in the library at the same time as you, simply waiting for you to go away!"

Mr. Baker nodded. "Apparently Mr. Richards might take the children's suggestion and hire Detective Mortimer to work on the case."

"Isn't it strange that something was stolen last time we were here?" Granny Janet noted.

Abby nodded. "The last thing we need is to be seen as suspects."

"No," Mr. Baker shook his head. "I think we're too honest for that. Besides, if the thief was caught on camera, then we would also be on camera. It could work as an alibi."

"A what?" Tom asked.

"An alibi," Mr. Baker repeated. "It's something you can use to prove you were somewhere else when a crime happened."

"Do you know what went missing last time?" Mrs. Baker asked the children.

"Mr. Richards said it was an old document, but other than that, he didn't let out any information," Phil answered.

"If it's the same thief both times, the document must be related to the diaries," Mr. Baker said.

"That's just what I said to Mr. Richards," Phil said. "I thought the document would make a great clue, but he said the investigation was for the police only."

"That's understandable," Mrs. Baker nodded. "Public involvement could make things a lot more complicated."

"Why would a thief be so interested in Edward Jenkins?" Abby thought aloud, her brows lowered.

"Whoa, Abby, I know where this is going," Mr. Baker said.

"You want to believe his treasure is still out there," Mrs. Baker added.

"It might be," Abby said, a little embarrassed.

"And it could make sense," Andy said suddenly. "If Edward was rich, then why did he need a job from Lord Bracken? If he had treasure, he wouldn't have become the manager of his friend's estate."

"You have a point," Mr. Baker conceded uneasily.

Mrs. Baker laughed. "What if Mrs. Fielding was thinking about the wrong person, or was confused by a novel? Edward could have been as poor as a pauper, and Lord Bracken could have had pity on him. We can't go on a treasure hunt just because we want to believe the story told by a lady with Alzheimer's."

"That's it!" Grandfather Wilson exclaimed, clicking his fingers to emphasize his words. "We could make it our mission to find out about this man for Marge's sake. If the story she told is true, and part of her inheritance hasn't come to her, this could be our way of helping her keep her cottage."

"Yes!" Mr. Baker said, getting excited too. "The Bible teaches that we are to protect widows and orphans, and we can do that by looking into this story ourselves."

"All right," Mrs. Baker agreed.

"That means we'll have to do research that will take up some of our holiday. Are we up for that?" Mr. Baker asked.

The rest of the Bakers nodded eagerly. "Let's do what we can for Mrs. Fielding," Phil said.

"Of course, if there's nothing to back up the story, we'll leave it be," Mr. Baker said. "We don't want to *waste* time, but just find out if there's anything relating these burglaries to the treasure-tale of Edward Jenkins."

CHAPTER 7

The next morning, everybody awoke rather early despite the late and exciting night. Abby phoned Julie right after breakfast to ask if the thief had been caught or the diaries found.

"Nope," Abby told the others once she was finished on the phone. "Nothing has been discovered, and the police haven't been able to do much. The cameras picked up the thief, but apparently they don't reveal anything except that he opened the cabinet using a key and left the building by climbing out a window."

"Is Mr. Richards going to hire Detective Mortimer?" Mr. Baker asked.

"Yes, he is," Abby answered. "Julie said the detective is catching the next flight here."

"Well that's excellent," Mr. Baker said. "I know he'll do a great job. Let's split up today and do the most research that we can. Grandfather and I can look for information at Bracken Hall; maybe Mother, Abby, and Andy can go to the nearest library to see what information is there; and Granny, Phil, and Tom can go visit Mrs. Fielding in the hospital."

"That sounds like a good plan," Phil said. The twins nodded in agreement.

As soon as possible, they split up into their groups and went their separate ways. Mr. Baker and Grandfather Wilson drove off to Bracken Hall, Granny Janet prepared to drive Phil and Tom to the hospital, and Mrs. Baker headed to the library with the twins.

It was the same library she had spent hours at as a little girl, and Mrs. Baker thoroughly enjoyed the scenic walk there with the twins.

They soon entered the library, walking through upright, glass barriers and past self-service book-scanning booths.

"It's quite high-tech, isn't it?" Andy commented.

Mrs. Baker nodded. "It's changed a lot since my childhood. I hope there are at least *some* librarians around!"

Fortunately there were two helpful ladies at the inquiry desk, and one of them directed the Bakers to a book about Lord Bracken.

"There don't seem to be many books about him," the lady said apologetically. "If you need any more help, just let me know."

"Thank you," Mrs. Baker smiled, before pulling both books about Lord Bracken and Bracken Hall from the shelf. "Let's find a table where we can look through these books," she said.

****

Meanwhile, Granny Janet was leading Phil and Tom down the hallways of the hospital, following the directions of the man at reception.

Finally, they came to the room they were looking for. The door was open, and they stepped quietly inside. It was a moderately-sized hospital room, with a number of beds down either side of it. Some of the patients they passed were asleep, and others were reading magazines, watching TV, or staring at the ceiling.

Old Marge was one of those staring upwards, and she was in the second bed on the left side of the room. Granny Janet approached the bedside in her gentle manner, and Old Marge looked up to see who it was.

"Hello, Marge," Granny Janet smiled. "It's me, Janet, and I've brought two of my grandsons along. Do you remember Phil and Tom?"

Old Marge blinked at Janet, and then a smile spread across her face. "Janet. You've come to visit me." She looked over at the boys. "Pleased to meet you. You remind me of my brother Arthur," she said to Phil. "You know, Arthur used to tell me the most wonderful stories. But there was one story I could tell better than him, though he'd never admit it," she chuckled.

"Was it about Edward Jenkins?" Phil asked, hoping to jog the lady's memory.

"Yes! That's right!" she said, looking at Phil. "Do you know that story?"

"We don't know the end of it," Granny Janet said.

"Oh," Old Marge said slowly. "The end is quite sad. Can I tell you the beginning, rather?"

"Please tell us the part where Edward was captured by pirates, after he threw his treasure chest overboard," Phil said.

"All right," Old Marge nodded, settling into a comfortable position on her elbows and modulating her voice. "Edward's ship was stuck on the rocks, and he threw his chest into the ocean—do you know that part? Then I'll go from there.

"The sea gradually calmed, but the ship was well and truly stuck on rocks. Pirate ships began to appear, coming closer and ever closer, like a band of wolves circling a wounded deer, or like prowling sharks. At first, Edward was determined to give a fight, despite the dangers. In the crossfire that ensued, he was badly wounded in both legs, and the crew thought he was going to die.

"The ship's doctor did all he could to help, but he knew that proper medical attention was necessary, and so the crew ceased firing and raised a white flag. Before long, the pirates boarded the ship. Edward spoke bravely to them, saying that they could take what they liked so long as they did not harm any of the men on board."

Old Marge continued speaking, so smoothly and coherently that it didn't seem that it was her speaking at all, but rather a recorded voice, a speech that had been memorized and was simply playing itself back. That was when Phil got the idea to record her with the voice recorder on his Smartphone, which he quickly did.

"The pirates made prisoners of all the men. They took the expensive cargo and finally demanded a ransom for the prisoners. Once the ransom was paid, they set the men free.

"Edward was so shaken up by his experience and so near death from his wounds that he had to stay ashore for many months. One of his legs had to be amputated from the knee down, and his struggle to survive was a long, drawn-out one. His family had constant support from Lord Bracken, who was a loyal friend of Edward.

"When Edward finally started to recover, he had to spend much time resting. It was then that he mapped out the location of the rocks he had wrecked on, and therefore also the location of his treasure chest. He was also quite a keen artist and spent his time painting.

"His wife and Lord Bracken persuaded him to give up trading altogether, and to stay on land where pirates could never lay hold of him again. Edward partly wanted to go back and retrieve his treasure, but Lord Bracken persuaded him against such a dangerous venture, instead offering him position as manager of the Bracken estate.

"Because of his gratitude to Lord Bracken, Edward accepted the offer. He settled down to raise his three sons in the rural landscape, and he and his wife had two more sons there. All seemed peaceful, but as years passed, trouble began to brew beneath the surface."

There were voices at the door of the room as an assistant nurse entered, asking if any of the patients were hungry.

Phil looked anxiously at Granny Janet, and she understood his fear. Before they could do anything, she had come up to Old Marge's bed and interrupted the story.

"Excuse me, please. Can I get you anything to eat or drink?" she asked.

Old Marge blinked, her speech stopping abruptly. "Uh, what's that?"

"Can I get you anything to eat or drink?" she repeated.

"Um, a sand-shark would be nice."

The assistant nurse looked blankly at Old Marge, not sure what to say. Fortunately for her, a more experienced nurse came up just then.

"She wants a sand-shark," the assistant nurse whispered hurriedly to the other nurse.

Turning to Old Marge, the older nurse said, "A sandwich? Is that what you'd like?"

Old Marge just nodded, and then the two nurses went on their way, asking the rest of the patients what they'd like to eat.

Phil looked desperately at the elderly lady. He had forgotten to stop the recording on his Smartphone, and his hand held it limply.

"Trouble beneath the surface?" he asked. "What kind of trouble?"

Old Marge looked at him and blinked. She looked at Granny Janet, and then at Tom. "How nice of you to visit. Look at my flowers," she said, motioning to a bouquet of pink roses at her bedside.

"They're very beautiful," Granny Janet nodded.

Phil, in his desperation, remembered his Smartphone. "I know! I recorded you telling the story, now maybe if you hear the recording, you'll remember the rest of the story!"

He stopped the recording and hastily made the Smartphone play it back. "There," he said as Old Marge's voice began playing from the phone's speakers.

Old Marge chuckled as she heard herself speaking in the recording. "I sound quite different, don't I?"

"Listen to what you were saying, Marge," Granny Janet said.

Phil stopped the playback before the part where the nurse interrupted. "So what was the trouble brewing beneath the surface?" he asked again.

"Right," Old Marge nodded, moistening her lips, "I'll tell you. Five strong sons were born to Edward Jenkins, and when the oldest three were grown up, they began to get restless.

"It started with the eldest, Lloyd. He decided to find his father's treasure, and possibly avenge him by attacking the pirates. He set out, intending to return in a few weeks, but never came back. Word came that he had drowned in a storm. He'd always been the most sensible son, and everybody had assumed he would inherit everything when his father died, as was the custom of those times. Nobody had taken into account the possibility that he might die before his father.

"His unfortunate death meant that the next son, Albert, would be the heir. Albert and the next son, Henry, were close in age and fiery in disposition, and they had a disagreement over who should inherit the chest. The bad feelings escalated until the two of them had a fight over it, in which they both were killed. I suppose it just goes to show how much trouble was caused by that custom of the oldest son inheriting everything.

"Edward and his wife were understandably heartbroken over the loss of their three oldest sons. Lord Bracken, being the loyal friend that he was, wanted to end the strife in the family and thereby preserve the lives of the two remaining sons, Ernest and Francis."

Old Marge paused and leaned over to get a sip of water from the glass at her bedside. Meanwhile, Phil, Tom, and Granny Janet waited in suspense to hear Lord Bracken's intervention. Phil, in particular, was dreading the return of the nurses with Old Marge's "sand-shark" for lunch.

"He told Edward of his idea, to which Edward and his wife consented readily," she said, settling back comfortably onto the pillows, "Lord Bracken had the Jenkins family over for a grand supper, and afterwards they all went into his favorite gallery. 'Ernest and Francis,' he said to the two remaining sons, 'I know you are both sensible boys, and that you will submit to reason. You can see what strife and heartbreak your father's treasure has brought to your family. Your older brother Lloyd may have had honorable intentions, but they were not enough to keep him alive. Your brothers Albert and Henry were not content to rest at home, doing honest labor and building character. Rather, they wanted to live off the hard work of their father, and you can see where their greed has taken them.

"'And now I ask you, on behalf of your parents, and as a friend who only wants to see the well-being of your family, to leave off your hunt for your father's treasure. Let it become buried under the waves and sand, and just as deeply buried from your memory. Remain honest workers—be content with such things as you have, as the Good Book says. Please boys, consider this well: that the foolish son is a grief to his parents, but the wise son is a delight to them.'

"Ernest, the older son, needed some time to consider Lord Bracken's words, but he soon came to agree with them and solemnly promised not to go after the treasure, though he would one day inherit it. He also promised to advise his own children to do the same. Francis, the youngest son, made his promise even before Ernest did.

"Those two boys both kept their promises, thereby stopping the strife in the Jenkins family, and they settled down to do honest work. They made their own small fortunes and never regretted leaving the treasure at the bottom of the ocean.

"The story of the treasure has been passed down all those generations, including its solemn warning against greed. And that, I think, is the end of the tale," Old Marge said in conclusion.

"Has the promise passed down as well?" Phil asked, fascinated by the story.

"The promise?" Old Marge said, her eyes questioning.

"Did each generation have to promise not to go after the treasure?" Phil clarified.

"Oh, apart from the first two generations, I don't know."

"So the treasure might not be at the bottom of the ocean anymore?" Phil said, half as a statement and half as a question.

"Well I've never heard of anybody in my family finding it," Old Marge replied. "If somebody had, I'm sure we would know," she chuckled.

"Marge, you have done a wonderful job of remembering this much," Granny Janet praised. "Could you tell us if this story is a fact or more of a legend?"

"Oh, it's real," she said in a serious tone. "My own grandfather told me the story when I was just a little girl, and I would ask him to tell it again and again as I grew up. He would always make it sound so interesting. I would pretend I had never heard it before, and I'd ask the same questions every time."

Old Marge fell silent, and the only break in the stillness was the heavy breathing of a man asleep on a bed in the corner.

"Mrs. Fielding," Phil asked quietly, "do you have the map?"

"The map?" she asked.

"The map that Edward made," he said, his voice low.

"Oh no, of course not!" Old Marge replied. "Didn't I tell you? Lord Bracken persuaded Edward to lock the map away inside Bracken Hall so that nobody could go after the treasure, even if he wanted to."

Phil's jaw suddenly slackened, and he couldn't help drawing his breath in sharply. "Bracken Hall?" he muttered. He looked at Granny Janet, and she nodded slowly in understanding of his consternation.

"I think it's time for us to go now, Marge," Granny Janet said, trying to sound as calm as before. "We've been away from home quite a while, and I think Wilson might be getting hungry soon."

"Yes, yes, I quite understand," Old Marge nodded. "Thank you for letting me visit you. I'll come again soon."

Granny Janet looked sympathetically at Old Marge, who seemed to get quite muddled up in her vocabulary sometimes.

They walked out the room and through the hospital corridors in thoughtful silence. Then Granny Janet said, "Tom, you were such a good and quiet boy in there. Thank you."

"You're welcome," Tom replied. "Mrs. Fielding tells very interesting stories."

"She certainly does," Phil nodded. "I'm glad I got all that recorded so the others can hear it too." He paused. "What Mrs. Fielding said about Bracken Hall really got me thinking."

"Yes," Granny Janet nodded. "I wonder if the thief who has been lurking around knows that the map is locked up somewhere inside."

"That's just what I was thinking. Let's just hope it's still there."

Granny Janet nodded soberly.

CHAPTER 8

When they got home, they found the others in the living room. Mrs. Baker and the twins were back from the library, and were studying the books they had brought with them. Grandfather and Mr. Baker were doing research on their laptops.

"Hi there," Abby looked up and smiled as Phil, Granny Janet, and Tom entered the living room. "Did you discover anything?"

"Oh boy, we sure did," Phil nodded. The others looked up at the tone of his voice. "Mrs. Fielding finished Edward's story."

"Did she really?" Andy gasped.

"Tell us what she said!" Abby exclaimed.

"I recorded her on my phone, so you'll all be able to hear the story first-hand."

"Excellent!" Mr. Baker exclaimed.

Phil sat down, putting his phone's volume right up and playing the recording. The others listened in rapt attention as the tale unfolded, and they looked up disappointedly when the nurse interrupted.

"That's not the end, is it?" Mrs. Baker asked.

"Fortunately not, but it was a close call," Phil answered. "Mrs. Fielding only remembered what she had been saying when I played this clip back to her." He navigated onto the next recording and played that back as well, until the story was finished.

"So that's why the diaries were stolen!" Abby cried, her eyes wide. "The thief must be after the treasure too!"

"Yes, and maybe it was the map he stole the first time," Andy nodded.

"Does anybody else have anything to report back on?" Mr. Baker asked. "We were hoping to look up old records in the Bracken Hall library, but it was closed to the public."

"That's why I've been researching Edward Jenkins on my laptop," Grandfather Wilson said. "There's an article about him, which I've read through a few times, but no mention is made of treasure."

"Is there anything about his shipwreck?" Mrs. Baker asked.

"Oh yes, and it documents the loss of his leg in the battle with pirates. The article also mentions his wife and five sons who lived on Bracken Estate. Nothing here disagrees with Marge's story."

"Well that certainly indicates something about her abilities," Granny Janet said. "

"Yes," Abby replied. "Mother found some books at the library about Alzheimer's Disease, which I've been looking through. The disease is a very interesting topic to learn about."

"Could you tell us a bit about it?" Phil asked.

"Sure. The human brain is made of millions of nerve cells, which have tentacle-like structures called dendrites to connect them to each other. They send electrical impulses and chemicals to each other to perform the operations of memory, speech, vision, problem-solving, and so on.

"The current understanding is that various things can go wrong with the cells, causing them to die. This means there are gaps between the cells—missing connections. The result is different types of dementia, including Alzheimer's Disease.

"Dementia is usually progressive, meaning that the symptoms get worse as time passes. The brain basically shrinks as its cells die over the years. That's called atrophy. The symptoms vary depending on what area of the brain is dying."

"That is fascinating," Phil said.

"And scary!" Andy shuddered. "Imagine your brain shrinking."

"Fortunately, the causes of Alzheimer's aren't related to normal aging," Abby replied. "That's why not everybody gets it."

"We found some other books in the library," Mrs. Baker said, "and they were about Bracken Hall. We can't find anything in them about Edward Jenkins, though."

"Can you find any clues about a map locked away somewhere?" Mr. Baker asked.

Mrs. Baker looked over at Andy. "I can't think of anything I've read that would relate to that; have you?"

"No," Andy shook his head.

"I've been researching the coast of England," Mr. Baker said. "It seems pirates were a common scourge, and they plagued many areas. They did have their favorite spots, though." He stopped speaking suddenly, as though he had an idea, and looked up at Grandfather Wilson. "Did the article about Edward mention where the ship ran aground?"

"Ah yes, it did," Grandfather Wilson nodded. His eyes skimmed down the lines of writing on the laptop screen. "Merchant . . . next voyage . . large storm," he mumbled as he read down the page. "Here it is," he said. " 'His ship ran aground on rocks off the coast near the Lizard peninsula.'"

Mr. Baker furrowed his brow in concentration as he typed the words 'Lizard peninsula' into his search engine and then skimmed through the results.

"Well it seems a popular tourist destination," he muttered as he modified his search.

"Oh yes, it's a beautiful place," Granny Janet agreed.

"We might need to know a more exact location," Mr. Baker said.

Phil nodded. "We need Edward Jenkins's map."

"Should I phone Julie to ask when Detective Mortimer arrives?" Abby asked, getting up.

"Yes," Mr. Baker agreed.

Abby dialed Julie's mobile number. She answered after just a few rings.

"Hello?"

"Hi, Julie, it's Abigail Baker speaking."

Julie laughed.

"What is it?" Abby asked.

"You don't really have to introduce yourself," Julie explained. "Your accent does that for you."

"Oh, I see," Abby laughed. "Well I was just phoning to ask when Detective Mortimer is arriving. We'd like to see him."

"He caught the earliest flight he could, so he'll arrive this afternoon. I think he'll go straight to police headquarters after he lands and then come over to the Hall to investigate."

Once Abby had related that news. Mr. Baker had the idea to invite the detective for supper as an opportunity to tell him what they had discovered about the case.

Detective Mortimer arrived at the grandparents' house that night at seven o'clock sharp, his perceptive eyes darting around as they always did when he was busy with a case. He was a thin, wiry man of average height with a high forehead, large eyes, prominent cheekbones, and reddish-brown hair and a mustache.

He put out his hand to shake Mr. Baker's. "Thank you for inviting me," he said. "It's a pleasant coincidence that we are both in England at the same time."

"And puzzling out the same mystery," Mr. Baker added with a laugh.

Phil shook his hand. "It's good to see you again, Detective."

"You too, Philip."

The detective was ushered into the living room, introduced to Grandfather Wilson and Granny Janet, and given a comfortable seat.

Supper was served, and it was a creamy risotto with mushrooms, sun-dried tomatoes, and spinach, topped with Parmesan cheese. The conversation at the table was pleasant, and as soon as the food was finished, the ladies disappeared with the dirty dishes and returned with cups of coffee for the adults and cocoa for the young people.

"It seems like an interesting case at Bracken Hall," Detective Mortimer said, coming to the point quickly. "Could you tell me what have you discovered so far?"

Phil leaned forward in his seat. "Detective, we believe the thief at Bracken Hall might have stolen an ancient treasure map." He started right at the beginning of the story, telling the detective all about their first visit with Marge, the missing diaries at Bracken Hall, and what they had discovered that morning.

"I can send you the recordings of Mrs. Fielding's narrations, if you'd like," he finished.

"Yes, those may be very useful," the detective replied. "Do you think the thief could be after Edward Jenkins's treasure?"

"That seems likely," Phil said. "All the clues we've found and research we've done seems to lead to Cornwall."

The detective nodded slowly. "Reason leads me to ask if you are certain this treasure has not already been discovered?"

"I've been wondering the same thing," Mr. Baker muttered in agreement.

"All we have to go by is Mrs. Fielding's word that it hasn't been found," Phil answered, "but I don't see why a thief would steal diaries if there was nothing to gain by it."

Detective Mortimer tapped his fingers on his cup before speaking again. "May I ask what your involvement in this case is? Is it just that a treasure hunt has captured your imaginations?"

"No, it's more than that," Mr. Baker said. "You see, Marge has Alzheimer's Disease. She lives in the next cottage."

Grandfather Wilson nodded. "Her daughter Sue says she's too busy to look after Marge, and would like her to go into a care home. The idea is to rent out Marge's cottage to cover the expenses."

"Yes," Mr. Baker resumed. "Marge is upset at the idea of leaving her home, and this is where we come in. We believe that if there is a treasure out there that is hers by inheritance, we should find it for her. That way, she'll have the finances to stay in her cottage and employ a care-worker, since no family members can look after her."

Detective Mortimer looked thoughtfully at Mr. Baker. It was a tense moment, as everybody in the room was sure the detective would think the idea was a crazy one. Phil feared the detective would think they only believed in the existence of a treasure because they wanted to.

The tapping of his fingers slowed to a stop. Then he opened his mouth to speak, a faint smile around his eyes. "So when are you leaving for Cornwall?"

"You believe there might be a treasure?" Phil almost gasped.

"It wouldn't be the first time," Detective Mortimer replied. "Less imaginative detectives might tell you what a far-fetched idea this is, but what they fail to remember is that criminals have imaginations too. You might never know the end of the story unless you investigate it. You are on holiday and have time to do that, knowing that you are potentially going down a rabbit trail."

"If we don't do a little digging, I know we'll always regret it!" Abby added excitedly.

"Will you come with us?" Phil asked.

Detective Mortimer shook his head. "I have been hired by Mr. Richards to catch his thief, and employers don't look too kindly on rabbit trails. Besides, if there are any criminals out looking for treasure, the presence of a detective will immediately alert them to danger. You, on the other hand, can pose as an innocent tourist family."

"Could we stay in contact by phone, or might the calls be tracked?" Phil asked.

"Whoever is behind the burglaries probably knows I am on the case," Mortimer replied, "and therefore any communication with me will have to be carefully calculated. Coded e-mails might be a wiser choice than phoning."

"Detective," Mrs. Baker began uneasily, "I'd rather not go on a wild goose chase just for the fun of it. How likely do you think it is that we'll find Edward

Jenkins' treasure?"

The detective paused. "I don't think it extremely likely that you will find the treasure. I do, however, have a sneaking suspicion that you'll find other people who are looking for it. And that," he paused for effect, "would be very useful."

Mrs. Baker frowned. "Will that be safe?"

"Perhaps not. But I can't think of any other family who would take that risk to help an elderly widow. If that treasure gets stolen, she will be defrauded of her inheritance. If you don't do anything, I don't imagine anybody else will."

"You have a good point," Mr. Baker said.

"I advise you to think about it," Detective Mortimer said, getting up to go. "Tomorrow is Sunday; why not use the afternoon to have a good ponder?" He pulled on his smart, black coat and buttoned it up. "Are you going to the local church in the morning? Then I'll see you there. Thank you again for the delicious meal. Goodbye."

****

The next afternoon, Abby found her father in the living room in deep thought.

"Knock, knock," she said softly.

"Come in," Mr. Baker said, being aroused from his thoughts.

Abby went and sat down beside him. "Father, I'd like to ask you something."

"Go ahead," Mr. Baker replied encouragingly.

"Father, what exactly does the Bible say about widows?"

"Well, Abby, that's a good question. Again and again, the Bible mentions widows and orphans as people we should protect. It tells us that God wants us to make provision for them, and that He hates it when they are unjustly treated. Even though we're not judges or magistrates, we can obey this command in the ways we can, with the people we know."

Abby frowned. "Shouldn't Mrs. Sue Richards and other relatives be looking after Mrs. Fielding?" She looked up as Phil and Andy came in, and they paused, intrigued by the question.

Mr. Baker nodded. "Yes, but the problem in our day is that people around the world have lost the Lord's perspective on things. They don't see children as a heritage from the Lord, and they see elderly relatives as a burden and not a wealth of knowledge and wisdom. Maybe the Lord will use us to sow seeds in Sue and Peter's hearts.

"What Detective Mortimer said last night really made me think. We seem to be the only ones who believe that Old Marge is remembering something from her past. As the detective said, if we don't do what we can to ensure that her inheritance isn't stolen, maybe nobody else will. That's what has made me decide, and your mother agrees, that we should go to Cornwall to investigate. Just listen to this."

He looked down at the open Bible on his lap and moved his finger down the page. "This beautiful verse sums it all up. Isaiah 1:17 says, 'Learn to do good; seek justice, rebuke the oppressor; defend the fatherless, plead for the widow.' Does that answer your questions?"

Abby smiled. Her father always explained things carefully so others could understand them. "Yes, thanks, Father. That would be a good passage for me to memorize."

"So, when are we leaving for Cornwall?" Andy asked as Mrs. Baker walked in and sat down on the other side of Mr. Baker.

"Well," Mr. Baker said, looking at Mrs. Baker, "we were considering leaving early tomorrow morning."

"Really?" Abby gasped. "So soon! Well that's exciting! Are Granny and Grandfather coming too?"

"They haven't decided yet," Mrs. Baker answered. "It's quite a decision to make on such late notice."

"Yes," Mr. Baker nodded. "And somebody would have to look after Duke."

"Couldn't we take him with us?" Andy asked suddenly.

Mr. Baker shook his head slowly. "Andy, the journey is over six hours long; I don't think taking Duke would be a good idea."

"Have you booked accommodation yet?" Phil asked, getting excited too.

Mr. Baker laughed. "You should know your mother well enough by now to guess that she's got every detail organized in her mind."

Phil and the twins laughed.

"It's not booked yet," Mrs. Baker smiled. "I've just got my eye on a particular place that I'll book as soon as your father agrees about it."

"Where is the place?" Abby asked.

"Well," Mrs. Baker smiled, "it's a gorgeous little cottage in some rural countryside a few miles from Lizard Point."

"That's the southernmost tip of England, where a lot of ships were wrecked in the past," Mr. Baker explained.

"Yes," Mrs. Baker nodded. "We'll be staying in an old barn that's been converted into one of five holiday cottages situated on a little farm."

"That sounds great!" Phil said.

The twins agreed heartily.

"Now, you're going to have to pack carefully and thoughtfully, and not leave things to the last minute," Mr. Baker said, looking at Andy specifically. "We want to get an early start and leave at five in the morning. That means everything has to be packed before you go to sleep tonight."

"It also means I'll be coming around to wake you up at three thirty tomorrow morning," Mrs. Baker smiled.

"Three thirty!" Andy groaned.

"If we have six hours in the car, Andy, you'll have plenty of time to catch up on your beauty sleep," Phil remarked.

"This is such exciting news!" Abby exclaimed, jumping out of her seat. "I think I'll start packing right away."

CHAPTER 9

True to her word, at three thirty the next morning, Mrs. Baker crept into Abby and Tom's room and gently nudged Abby awake.

"Abby! Abby!" she whispered. "It's time to get up. Try not to wake Tom; he can sleep longer."

With Abby awake, Mrs. Baker headed next for the boys' room. There she had to be a lot noisier, especially in Andy's case.

The Baker siblings got up, dressed, and came into the living room, being greeted by the strong smell of filter coffee. The adults were all sitting around the table, sipping coffee and talking in hushed voices.

"Good morning," Granny Janet smiled as her grandchildren entered. A volley of whispered "Good Mornings" flew around the room, sounding mysterious.

"Please sit down," Grandfather Wilson welcomed, trying to restrain his naturally sonorous voice.

"Thank you," Abby responded, eyeing the muffins on a platter on the table.

Andy rested his forehead on his hands and yawned.

"Would you like some cocoa?" Mrs. Baker asked merrily as he looked up again, his eyes puffy and lips pouting from sleep.

"Cocoa? Yes, please," he nodded tiredly.

Mrs. Baker poured three cups of cocoa, diluting them well with milk and sugar.

"Help yourself to muffins," Granny Janet smiled. "Those ones are apple strudel muffins, and those are blueberry."

"Apple strudel muffins?" Abby repeated as she chose one. "That sounds interesting. Mmm, they're delicious!" she said as she took a bite after saying grace.

"Are you coming with us?" Phil asked his grandparents.

Grandfather Wilson shook his head. "It's too late notice for us old folks," he chuckled. "Besides, I think I'm going to get my foot seen to. It's not healing as quickly as it should."

"Also," Granny Janet said, "I don't think I'm up to driving such a long distance, and I feel that Wilson and I should be here to look after Marge."

"I see," Phil nodded. "Yes, then we don't have to worry about her."

Mrs. Baker looked anxiously at her watch. "Dear, it's past four o'clock. I think you and the boys should start packing the car soon."

"Yes," Mr. Baker agreed. "We'll start at four thirty. Eat up, boys."

Once the boys were finished with their muffins and cocoa, they started packing the suitcases into the car. In the meantime, Mrs. Baker woke Tom up and helped him get ready, and Abby and Granny Janet packed food for the journey.

They all said fond farewells to Granny Janet and Grandfather Wilson, prayed for traveling mercies, and then at five o'clock sharp they climbed into their car and pulled away from the familiar cottage.

Abby settled down into her seat and pulled her pillow closer in an effort to get comfortable. The sky was dark, but faint color was appearing in the east, announcing the coming of dawn. She looked out the window for a minute, resting her head against the pillow, and then closed her eyes.

The drive to Cornwall was a very long one, and the Bakers had to stop a few times for a chance to walk around a little.

Andy excitedly pointed out Stonehenge as they drove past, and he managed to snap a few photos of it.

It was about lunchtime when Tom announced suddenly, "I need the bathroom."

Mr. Baker had taken a wrong turn when the SatNav system momentarily blanked out, and the Bakers were driving through a seaside town. Quaint houses hugged the seashore, and a small harbor they passed was crowded with motorboats and yachts.

"Okay, Tom," Mr. Baker said. "I'll stop as soon as I can."

Mr. Baker found a parking area, and Mrs. Baker headed with Tom to the public toilets nearby. When they came back, the Bakers decided to explore the town and find a place to eat the lunch Abby and Granny Janet had prepared that morning.

"Cornwall is just how Grandfather described it!" Abby laughed as they strolled through town. "Look at all the old shops—a candy shop, a surf shop. . . "

"A Cornish pasty shop," Andy added.

"Yes!" Abby nodded with a laugh.

They walked down the cobbled streets and peered through the windows of the shops they passed. Finally, they stopped outside a sweet shop with a sign that read "Organic Cornish Ice-Cream Sold Here! The Best in Cornwall!"

"Should we get some organic Cornish ice-creams after lunch?" Mr. Baker asked his wife, chuckling as he read the sign.

"They're the best in Cornwall!" Abby added.

"Oh yes, I'd love to," Mrs. Baker said.

They found a sunny spot near the beach and ate their delicious roast-beef sandwiches. After enjoying every bite, they headed back to buy ice-creams.

They entered the small shop, which was a cozy refuge from the sea breezes outside. A man with round spectacles greeted them from behind the counter.

"Good afternoon," the man said.

"Hello," Mr. Baker replied.

"Can I help you at all?" the man asked.

Abby's eyes traveled around the walls of the shop, running over the array of sweets for sale.

"Yes, please," Mr. Baker nodded. "We'd like some of your organic Cornish ice-creams."

"Here they are," the man said, motioning to the ice cream counter. Tubs of ice cream of many colors and flavors stood behind glass, just waiting to be chosen.

"What would you like?" Mr. Baker asked, looking at Mrs. Baker.

"What's the most popular?" she asked the man.

"Probably vanilla," he answered.

"I think I'll try your pistachio, please."

"Triple chocolate looks tasty," Phil said in answer to his father's look.

"Mmm! Bubblegum flavor, please," Andy chose with a grin.

"Uh, I don't know," Abby deliberated. "They all look good. I'd like to try butterscotch, please."

"And you, Tom?" Mr. Baker asked.

"Please, can I have peppermint?"

"Certainly. I'd like coffee flavor, please," he said, turning to the man behind the counter. He paused, a frown creasing his forehead. "Is it true that there were many shipwrecks around here?" he asked.

The man nodded. "Oh yes. This was a very dangerous place because of hidden reefs. People go diving to see the wrecks."

"That's interesting," Phil muttered.

"Tourists love to have their imaginations captured that way, and they love to hear about pirate hide-outs, smugglers, and buried treasure," the man said with a laugh.

Just then, the door opened, and three burly men entered the shop. Immediately, the mysterious air snapped and daydreams were sucked back into their rightful place.

"Here are your ice-creams," the man said as he placed the last one in the stand on the counter-top. "That's £14.40, please."

Mr. Baker delved into his wallet and pulled out some bank notes and coins, which took him a short while to decipher. He handed the ice-creams to his family members, before thanking the man and turning to go.

"You should probably visit Lizard Peninsula if it's shipwrecks you're interested in," the man called after them.

"Thank you," Mr. Baker replied.

"He was very helpful," Mrs. Baker commented as they walked along the pavement towards some benches with a view of the sea.

"Yes. Let's get settled into our cottage, and perhaps we can explore Lizard Point tomorrow," Mr. Baker said.

"That's just what I was thinking," Mrs. Baker said.

Once they had finished their ice-creams, they headed back to the car to resume their journey. About an hour later, they drove down a little road and turned into a cluster of old farm buildings. The sun was shining, casting a happy glow on the bright flowers in the flower-beds.

A blonde, middle-aged lady came out of a farmhouse and walked up to the car. "Hello," she greeted in a friendly voice. "Have you come to stay in Riverside Cottage?"

"Yes, we have," Mr. Baker nodded. "I'm Charles Baker; this is my wife Alice, who phoned yesterday."

"Yes, I remember. I'm Anne."

The Bakers all climbed out of the car and introduced themselves to Anne.

"I'm pleased to meet you all. Shall I show you around the cottage?" she asked.

"Yes, please," Mrs. Baker nodded eagerly.

Anne led the way to a quaint barn conversion and unlocked the door. On stepping inside, the first thing the Bakers saw was the neat kitchen and equipment in it. The kitchen flowed into the dining area in an open-plan manner, and following on was the lounge with two comfortable sofas and a television. Upstairs were three large bedrooms and a very smart bathroom.

"I'll leave you to settle in," Anne said once she had seen the Bakers' pleased faces. "There are a dozen eggs in the kitchen from our chickens, and a jar of homemade marmalade. If you need anything, I'll be in the farmhouse opposite here."

They thanked Anne, and then began the arduous task of emptying the car, carrying suitcases upstairs, and unpacking clothes into the cupboards.

Mrs. Baker started orienting herself in the kitchen. "This is a lovely place, and Anne is very sweet," she commented.

The others nodded.

"Did Granny show you something about online shopping last night, Mother?" Abby asked.

"Yes," Mrs. Baker answered. "We ordered groceries, which should be delivered any time between now and four o'clock."

Only a little later was there a knock at the door, and Mrs. Baker opened it to see a man in uniform standing behind a stack of three large, plastic crates.

"Good afternoon!" the man greeted in a strong accent. "Would you like me to carry these into the kitchen?"

The groceries were carried into the kitchen one crateful at a time, and the man had to make a few trips to his truck to return the empty crates and come back with full ones.

Finally, when the last crate had been emptied, Mrs. Baker signed her name on the man's touch-screen device to confirm that the delivery had taken place, and he drove away to his next destination.

There was a flurry of shopping bags and busy hands as the children helped Mrs. Baker pack away the groceries while Mr. Baker had a well-deserved nap.

Afterwards, they had a look around the small farm they were staying on. There was a decent-sized back garden, separated from a field and gurgling stream by a low, stone wall. There was also a chicken coop, where five or six chickens clucked happily. On the other side of the cottage, beyond the little road, was a large field stretching into the distance.

The rest of the day passed pleasantly and ended off with a walk along the beach, although in the children's case, that walk turned into a race. There was something so exhausting about the sea air that by the time the Bakers got home, they only had enough energy to eat supper, read the Bible, and then fall fast asleep.

CHAPTER 10

The next morning, the Bakers got up bright and early. They had a delicious breakfast of soft-boiled egg and soldiers, the "soldiers" being strips of buttered toast. Earl Grey tea and marmalade toast finished off the meal nicely, and when the Bakers had all eaten as much as they needed, they began the drive down to Lizard Point.

When they finally arrived at the car park, they were astounded by the spectacular ocean view, bounded on the left by a steep hill. Great Black-backed Gulls were everywhere, and the Bakers were quite surprised by their large size. The family quickly started walking seaward, down towards the shops and café.

The Bakers reached the edge of a sheer cliff face with waves pounding down below. Then they climbed up the steep hill to the left, following a path along the cliff edge until they came to the top.

"Wow!" Abby gasped. "There's almost a 360 degree view of the ocean from here!"

"Goodness, it's so windy!" Mrs. Baker cried as her hat nearly flew away.

Abby zipped her jacket tighter and pulled her hair into a ponytail in an effort to keep it from being blown around by the wind.

"Let's continue walking and see if we can find a shore," Mr. Baker called, leading onwards.

They followed him, and on and on they walked. They traipsed up and down hills exposed to the wind, around sheltered bends, and beside cliff edges until they were all exhausted. Tom had long since become too tired to go on, and was clinging to his father's back.

They came to the top of a plateau, where the boys went as close as they dared to the cliff edge, inching forward on their stomachs and peering down into the frothy waves below.

They continued down the hill, and then came to a place where the path split in two directions. Going straight would mean continuing beside the cliff edge, but going left would mean going towards the sea, down a mysterious path with high rock walls on either side.

"Let's see what's this way," Mr. Baker said as he entered the comfortably sheltered path.

The path descended in roughly hewn steps and around a corner, so that Abby couldn't see the sea or where the path was taking them. They descended until the steps gave way to a rough slope with a strong wire cable running down the side of it.

"Grab the cable," Phil said from behind, as Abby nearly slipped. She took his advice, and proceeded cautiously forward around the last of the corner.

Once she had turned the last bend, she saw where the path was taking them. Several paces forward, the path suddenly dropped five feet to a pebble beach bordered by cliffs.

"This place is amazing!" Abby gasped.

"It sure is," Phil agreed. "Andy, have you got photos?"

"Plenty!" was the reply from in front of Abby.

"Father, how do we get down to the beach?" Phil called.

"There's a ladder here," Mr. Baker replied.

They watched as Mr. Baker carefully squatted down so Tom could climb off his back. Then, with one hand holding the cable, he turned around and lowered himself onto the ladder. A few seconds later, he was safely on the pebbles and motioning for Tom to follow. Then it was Mrs. Baker's turn to be helped onto the ladder.

Once they had all descended the ladder, they found themselves on a small, rough beach that was strewn with rocks of all sizes. The rock formations and pillars were well worn by the battering and eroding force of the sea.

"When the tide comes in," Mr. Baker observed, "this shore is probably covered in water."

"That's not a very comforting thought," Mrs. Baker said, eyeing the cliff walls behind them.

"Father," Andy began, "Could I go and explore the rock pools over there?"

He pointed to some rocks at the far left edge of the beach, which the seawater nearly reached.

"All right, son," Mr. Baker replied.

Somehow, the thought of rock pools caught everybody's interest. They all followed Mr. Baker and Andy and headed towards the left corner of the cove.

The rock pools were full of life. Little fish darted around in them, and barnacles were everywhere. Sea snails sucked themselves securely onto the walls, and a couple of crabs were discovered.

Andy, the most adventurous and the most easily bored of the group, had climbed over the rocks the others were exploring. He was walking along a narrow strip of pebbles which the seawater didn't quite reach, bordered on the side by a high cliff face.

"Ahoy!" he cried to the others. "It looks like there's a cave in the rock wall just here. Come and look!"

Mr. Baker was the first to join Andy at the spot, followed by Phil and Abby.

"It looks like a passage!" Phil exclaimed. "I think I could fit in there quite comfortably."

"Andy, do you have your torch here?" Mr. Baker asked. "Shine the light in there, so we can see how far the cave goes."

Andy wasted no time in getting his torch out and beaming the light into the naturally formed passage. "It goes a really long way!" he said as he peered in.

"It looks like it," Mr. Baker nodded.

"Can we explore it, Father? Please?"

Mr. Baker eyed the sea level for a moment. "All right. But we're going to have to be quick. I don't want us to be caught by a rising tide."

"I'll stay out here to warn you when the tide starts coming in," Abby volunteered.

"Great idea," Mr. Baker said. "Okay, Andy, you lead the way."

"Thanks Abs," Phil patted her shoulder as he followed Mr. Baker into the cave.

Andy's torchlight bounced off the walls of the passage as he led the way inside. It stretched on for a surprising distance. Each breath seemed to echo, and every footstep made a crunching noise on the pebbly tunnel floor.

Andy came to a sudden halt as the passage ended.

"So that's it?" Mr. Baker asked, preparing to turn around.

"No, it isn't," Andy breathed. "Look at this!"

He shone his torch to the right, revealing another cave-like passage. He was about to enter it when Mr. Baker turned his face towards the cave entrance. "Abby!" he called. "How's the tide?"

Abby heard her father's question as it bounced off the rock walls of the passage. She leaned into the cave, cupped her hands around her mouth, and replied, "Fine."

"Thank you!" Mr. Baker replied. "Go on, Andy."

Andy ventured into the passage to the right. It went straight ahead for quite a while, and then curved right before suddenly opening into a wide cave, which looked out onto another pebble beach.

"We've discovered another beach," Andy said. "I'm sure it's just a little distance from the one we were last at."

"I'm not so sure," Mr. Baker frowned. "To me, it seems to face a completely different angle to the first beach."

"There are people there," Phil pointed, his voice hushed. "I just saw somebody appear from behind that corner of rock, at the water's edge."

"They're probably other adventurers who discovered the passage," Mr. Baker said. "Let's go and see what's over there."

They walked through the cave, and where it opened out into broad daylight were three large men in wetsuits preparing to launch a motorboat onto the water. They looked up in surprise at Mr. Baker and the boys.

"Hello," Mr. Baker said to the men, taking a step forward. "My sons and I were exploring and found this cove. I'm quite interested in diving to see the shipwrecks off the coast. Are you with a diving company?"

The men looked at each other, and then one of them replied in a rough English accent, "I'm sorry mate, but we can't help you. Your best bet is to go to one of the tourist information spots. They can tell you where to find whatever you're looking for."

"All right," Mr. Baker nodded. "Thank you very much."

They watched the men launch the boat into the water, and then Mr. Baker said, "I guess we'd better be heading back. I don't want your mother to get anxious about us."

They went back the way they'd come, down the two passages and towards the original beach. Already, water was lapping gently at the passage entrance.

Abby was still standing outside the mouth of the cave when they came out. "Oh!" she sighed when she saw them. "I'm relieved you're back. I was calling about the rising tide, but couldn't hear a reply."

"I'm sorry we startled you," Mr. Baker said as they walked back to the rock pools where Mrs. Baker and Tom were waiting rather anxiously. "That passage leads to another beach. We saw three divers go out in a boat," he said.

"I'm sure those were the three men we saw at the ice cream shop yesterday," Phil said.

"Really?" Mr. Baker asked. "I didn't pay attention to what they looked like."

"I'm hungry," Tom said.

"I've got a pack of oat biscuits in my pocket," Mrs. Baker said, "but shouldn't we leave this beach before the tide rises any higher? Already I'm getting nervous."

Mr. Baker nodded.

They all climbed the ladder and went back up the path sheltered by rock walls. It was only then that Abby noticed the lush, green plants growing on the walls. When they reached the top, and re-emerged onto the open hillside, Mrs. Baker handed around the biscuits which they ate hungrily.

"There—is that the divers' boat?" Andy asked suddenly, pointing out to sea.

The others followed his gaze. "Yes, it must be," Mr. Baker answered.

"Father, are you really thinking of going diving to see the shipwrecks off the coast?" Phil asked.

"I'm considering it," Mr. Baker nodded. "If Edward Jenkins's ship was wrecked here, his chest should be somewhere nearby."

"Yes, near his ship, I suppose," Mrs. Baker added.

"Oh," Andy muttered, "but if there are so many wrecks around here, how will we know which is the right one?"

The others frowned in thought.

"Don't you think the chest might have been found by one of the many tourists who come diving every year?" Abby asked.

"Yes, it could have been," Mr. Baker answered, "but I don't know where else to look if not at the bottom of the ocean."

They got home late that evening, tired out. They ate supper, had Bible reading, and then Tom got ready for bed. Phil checked his e-mails and found a message from Detective Mortimer.

"I've got a strange message from the detective," he muttered with a frown.

"What does it say?" Abby asked curiously.

"It says, 'Hope you have a Lovely outing on koast, out under trees.'"

"What?" Andy said. "Can I read it, Phil?"

"Sure," Phil nodded.

"That doesn't sound like Detective Mortimer."

"Look, he misspelled 'coast' and capitalized 'lovely,'" Abby pointed out. "Maybe it's not really the detective. It could be somebody pretending to be him."

"It's his e-mail address," Phil replied. "Somebody would've had to hack into his account to be able to do that. And, knowing the detective, he's probably got a very sophisticated password."

"Maybe he just made a typo because he was in a hurry," Andy suggested.

"Or maybe he did it on purpose," Phil said, narrowing his eyes as he re-read the short e-mail. "I remember him saying something about preferring coded e-mails to phone calls. Maybe that 'k' is in there to make us know there's more to the message than meets the eye."

Mr. Baker came over to see as well.

"If we take the first letter of every word, does that make anything meaningful?" Phil wondered aloud. "H—Y—H—A—L—O—O—K—O—U—T. Look out!"

Abby gasped, moving in for a closer look.

"Look out for what?" Mr. Baker asked. "Let's send him a coded message back, asking what he means."

Phil began typing the opening lines of his e-mail, and then stopped to consider how to code the question.

"Let's just send in code the two words 'what for,'" Mr. Baker said.

"So first we have W," Andy said. "What about 'We Have Asked Travis, For Our R...'? Hmm, I can't think of something with R."

"It could be 'We Have Arrived Today....'" Abby suggested, her voice trailing off. "No, that doesn't work. We arrived yesterday."

"That's still a good suggestion," Mr. Baker said.

"Yes!" Phil nodded. "After all, Detective Mortimer put a mistake in there to make us notice his code, so he'll notice our code if he sees our mistake in there."

"All right," Andy joined. "So 'We Have Arrived Today, and'—it would have to be the 'and' symbol so he doesn't think it's part of the code—'& Found Our Rooms.' What about that?"

"Great!" Mr. Baker said.

Phil quickly typed those words, and then read the e-mail out.

" 'Hi there Detective,

Thank you, we've been having a great time so far. Cornwall really is a beautiful place.

We have arrived today & found our rooms.

God bless,

Phil and family'"

He looked up from the screen. "How is that?"

"Great," Mr. Baker said. "Send it off, and let's see what comes back."

They received a reply just a few minutes later. "That was quick!" Phil exclaimed as he opened the e-mail. His eager expression turned to a frown. "He's written this: 'They have underestimated Gary's skills.' Then the rest of his message is in gibberish—I can hardly read it."

"Give it a try, Phil," Mrs. Baker encouraged.

"All right. 'Haigiraiged maigen aigare aigaftaiger thaige traigeasaigure,'" he stammered out the words.

"What?" Andy spluttered. "He really wrote that?"

"He must have dropped something onto his keyboard," Mrs. Baker suggested.

"If so, why didn't he clear that before sending the e-mail?" Abby frowned. "Do you think it's another language? Maybe it's Cornish."

"I have no idea," Phil shook his head. "Well let's see what the English part of his message is. T-H-U-G-S. Thugs!"

"Detective Mortimer is warning us of thugs?!" Mrs. Baker exclaimed. "Is that all we can figure out?"

"Hmm," Mr. Baker sighed, leaning forward as he scanned the words.

"Those other words might be some kind of explanation," His voice trailed off as he straightened up and rubbed the back of his neck.

"Taking the first letter of every word doesn't make sense," Andy noted.

"What about every two letters?" Abby wondered. "H—i—i—i—e—no, that can't be it," she shook her head.

"Maybe the first two letters of every word make something," Phil suggested. "Ha—ma—ai—ai—th—tr."

"Well that's hopeless," Andy concluded.

Mr. Baker again bent over to study the coded message. Suddenly he exclaimed, "Oh, I've got it!"

"What is it, Father?" Phil asked quickly.

"It's a code or language game called 'Aigy Paigy,' in which the letters 'aig' are inserted before every vowel combination in a word," Mr. Baker answered. "Let's look at the first word—'Haigiraiged.' Taking out every 'aig' in that word makes 'h-ir-ed.' The first word is 'hired.' Next is 'maigen.' 'M-en.' 'Aigare aigaftaiger thaige traigeasaigure'—are aft-er th-e tr-eas-ure. Hired men are after the treasure."

Mrs. Baker's eyebrows shot up, and Phil looked incredulous as he scribbled down the message on a piece of paper.

"Detective Mortimer first told us to look out, and then he told us that there are thugs after the treasure," Mr. Baker said. "We're obviously not the only ones out here looking for it."

"And that means they might find it first!" Abby said, her eyes wide.

"Yes," Mr. Baker nodded. "To have any chance of beating them to it, we would need to know exactly where it is."

Phil drew in his breath sharply. "The divers from yesterday! They were out diving in the ideal location for a shipwreck—and they might have been the thugs Detective Mortimer was warning us about!"

"You could be right," Mr. Baker said, the realization hitting him.

"After all, they were in a secret cove," Phil said.

"And they weren't with a diving company," Andy added. "Besides, they weren't too happy to have us around."

"If they went diving yesterday," Abby gasped, "then they've probably already found the treasure!"

"Oh no!" Mrs. Baker exclaimed.

"Phil, we have to ask Detective Mortimer if he knows whether or not the thugs have found the treasure yet," Mr. Baker ordered.

"Yes," Phil nodded quickly. "How should I code that?"

"We'll use Aigy Paigy, just like he did," Mr. Baker answered. "Let me type it in." His fingers started flying over the keyboard as he wrote the message. In the end, the e-mail read:

'Hi Detective,

Thanks for your previous message. Haigave thaige thaigugs faigound thaige traigeasaigure yaiget?'

"Father, that was quick!" Phil said. "Even I can't work that message out, and I know the cipher!"

They waited a while for a reply from Detective Mortimer, but none came.

"What are we going to do?" Mrs. Baker asked in agitation.

"The only thing I can think of is to go back to Lizard Point tomorrow," Mr. Baker said.

"Maybe we can go diving to make sure the treasure *isn't* there," Abby said without thinking.

"Diving might be a waste of time," Mr. Baker replied. "We don't have Edward Jenkins's map to tell us where to look."

"Will we leave first thing tomorrow morning?" Mrs. Baker asked.

Mr. Baker nodded. "Yes. As early as we can."

"All right, kids, you heard that," Mrs. Baker said. "It's already late, and we're going to need all the sleep we can get."

They hurried to get ready for bed, and an hour later the house was quiet.

Abby lay awake for some time, unable to get rid of the sense of urgency inside her. Thoughts whirled around in her mind. *Who are the thugs? Where are they now? Have they found the treasure yet? What will we do if they have? Are we too late?*

Her mind went back to the passage she had been memorizing. *'Learn to do good; seek justice, rebuke the oppressor; defend the fatherless, plead for the widow.' Plead for the widow.*

Then a realization struck her. *We can do all those things to our utmost, but the outcome is in the Lord's hands. Thank you, Lord, that it's in Your hands and not mine! Thank you that it's not up to me to make everything turn out right!*

CHAPTER 11

T he Bakers woke up early the next morning, like clockwork. They got dressed into suitable clothes for the windy outing that awaited them, and quickly ate their breakfast and did the washing up.

"Phil, have you got a new message from the detective?" Mr. Baker asked.

Phil had just opened his e-mail account. "Yes. It seems the thugs haven't got the treasure yet!"

"What did he say?" Andy asked.

"He just wrote 'Number 0,' so I'm guessing the first letter—N—coupled with the number 0 spells 'no.'"

"That's great news!" Mrs. Baker said.

"It sure is," Mr. Baker agreed. "Phil, bring your Smartphone with you in case we need to stay in touch with Detective Mortimer."

Very soon afterwards, the Bakers climbed into the car, their imaginations ready for whatever might happen.

Eventually, Andy broke the thoughtful silence. "Father, could you please tell us again how 'Aigy Paigy' works?"

"Yes, sure," Mr. Baker said. "Add the letters 'aig' before every vowel or vowel combination in a word. For example, take the word 'mother.' The word has two vowels—'o' and 'e.' If I add 'aig' before the vowels, the word would become 'M- aig—oth—aig—er. Maigothaiger."

"So my name would be...?" Abby finished with a confused look.

"Your nickname, A-bb-y would be Aig-a-bb-aig-y," Mr. Baker said slowly as he figured it out in his own mind. "Aigabbaigy."

The twins burst out laughing.

"What would I be?" Tom asked eagerly.

"Thomas would be Thaigomaigas—Taigom for short."

Half an hour later, they got out of their car in the Lizard Point parking lot. They walked down past the café together and up the steep hill. Phil quickly checked his e-mails on his Smartphone once more.

"No more news," he shook his head disappointedly.

"Maybe you should stay here," Mr. Baker said in thought as he considered the commanding view of the ocean. He dropped his voice. "You can keep an eye on the horizon for the divers. Call me if you see them or hear from the detective."

****

"The journey seems shorter today than it was last time," Abby thought aloud as they walked down the rough stone steps and slope sheltered by the two huge rock walls.

"This time we know where we're going," Andy pointed out. "Last time we were just following our noses."

One by one, they climbed down the ladder onto the pebbled beach.

"Father, can I see that cave you explored last time?" Abby asked. "The tide seems to be out pretty far."

"All right," Mr. Baker nodded. "Andy, would you go with your sister, please?"

"Yes, Father," he agreed. "Come on," he said, leading the way toward the rock pools.

Abby followed him over the slippery rocks and then back onto pebbles and sand beside the sheer, towering cliff face.

"Do you have your torch?" she asked as they stood at the mouth of the cave.

"As always," Andy grinned as he took it out and switched it on.

He led the way down the naturally formed passage. Apart from the torchlight, the only relief from the close darkness was the light of the cave's entrance, which looked very small and far away.

"This looks like a dead end," Andy whispered, "but the cave continues to the right. Eventually it opens out onto another beach."

The tunnel grew faintly lighter as they walked further onwards, and finally it curved and opened widely into a large cave with a beach further out.

Andy was about to step out of the tunnel and into the cave when he suddenly backed up and held out his arm to stop Abby from going forward. He immediately flicked off his torch and held his breath.

Finally, he breathed again and whispered lightly, "The divers from yesterday," as an explanation for his behavior. Abby nodded in understanding, and then watched as her brother leaned forward to see around the corner. When he didn't move back again, Abby picked up the courage to peek around the corner too.

When she looked around, she saw two men in wetsuits pulling a boat ashore. Another man in a wetsuit stood apart from them, nearer the tunnel, and he put a mobile phone to his ear. His hair was wet and plastered to his head, and he looked as though he had just been out swimming. A towel was in his other hand.

"Hello, Boss. It's Rich."

The suddenness of the man's rough address made Abby's heart skip a beat, and then race onward as she realized he was talking into his phone.

"Yeah, we've just come back in. It's not there."

Abby's ears pricked up as she realized that she and Andy might be overhearing something important.

"No, I'm telling you Boss, it's not there. We followed the map exactly." The man sighed angrily. "We went down yesterday and couldn't find it, we went down today and couldn't find it, and if you tell us to go down again tomorrow, we still won't find it—because it's not there!"

The speaker on the other end of the line must have been talking, because the man was silent for a while.

"But we haven't been looking in the same place all the time! We've searched a large area around the specific spot on the map, and still nothing has come up."

Finally, the man heaved another sigh. "Fine, we'll do that. Cheers." He turned to the other two men, who were emptying the boat of their diving gear.

"The boss says we've got to find the treasure, even if it means we have to do research. He says he's beginning to feel that we can't do the job right, and that we need professional help. You know what that means. We have to prove ourselves or lose money. Let's get into town and see what we can find out."

Andy tapped Abby's shoulder and then jabbed his thumb in the direction they had come from. As quietly and carefully as they could, they picked their way down the passage and eventually turned left down into the original one. They held their breath as long as they could because the cave was so echo-y.

When they got out into bright sunshine again, they each sucked in a lungful of air and ran back to their parents.

"We saw the divers from yesterday," Andy panted in broken phrases when he reached them. "They had just come back from diving again."

"You won't believe what happened," Abby gasped as she arrived after Andy. "We heard him talking on the phone to his boss."

"They can't find the treasure," Andy panted. "It's not where the map says it should be."

"They're going to look for clues in town," Abby finished.

"Wait—so the divers from yesterday are definitely the thugs Detective Mortimer warned us of?" Mr. Baker asked.

Andy nodded.

"And they're definitely looking for the same treasure as we are?" Mrs. Baker asked.

CHAPTER II

"It can only be," Abby gasped.

"Did they see you?" Mr. Baker inquired.

"No, we stayed hidden in the tunnel," Andy answered.

"Good. Well, we need to get back to Phil and start figuring things out as soon as possible," Mr. Baker said determinedly. "Let's go!"

They hurried back to the car park as fast as they could, and they were exhausted by the time they neared it. On their way, they passed Phil, who was in the same spot that they had left him in.

"Father," Phil smiled as he looked up. "Did you find anything?"

"We sure did. Any word from the detective?"

Phil nodded. "I've just finished deciphering this message from him. It says 'They have the map.' So they have an added head-start on us."

"Apparently they don't," Mr. Baker replied. "The treasure isn't where the map says it should be," he explained.

Phil's face took on a shocked expression, and he was about to ask a question when Mr. Baker said, "Come on, we've got to go right away. We'll explain things to you in the car."

They quickly climbed into the car and Mr. Baker started the engine. "So what did you discover?" Phil asked in intrigue as he snapped his seatbelt on.

"Andy and I went to look at the cave you explored yesterday," Abby answered. "The divers were on the other beach, and we overheard one of them talking on the phone to his boss. It seems the treasure is not in the place specified on the map."

"Well that's news! I hadn't counted on the map being unreliable."

"Whatever the case, they're going to town to look for clues to find where else the treasure could be," Andy said.

"Town?" Mrs. Baker said. "What clues do they intend to find in *town*?"

"I guess they mean to search old records or something," Mr. Baker answered.

"So should we look for old records while we have the time advantage?"

CHAPTER 11

Mrs. Baker asked.

"Absolutely," Mr. Baker nodded, turning the ignition of the car. "Let's find the nearest library. I'm sure the SatNav could direct us to one."

"Oh!" Phil said suddenly. "My phone. I've just got a message—and it's from Detective Mortimer. I think I'll be able to read what he says, though my battery is almost flat."

"Not again, Phil!" Andy said.

"What is the message?" Mr. Baker asked.

"It looks like 'Aigy Paigy' again," Phil replied. "Let's see; it's just one word—Llagoyd. So if I take the 'ag' out, it spells Lloyd."

"Lloyd?" Andy asked. "And that's supposed to be a clue?"

"Is it a town?" Abby suggested.

"Not that I know of," Mrs. Baker shook her head.

"The name rings a bell," Mr. Baker said with a frown. "I can't think of where it's from, though. Wait—isn't it the name of a bank? Lloyds TSB."

"Why would Detective Mortimer direct us to a bank?" Abby wondered.

"The treasure might be in the bank!" Tom suggested.

"You might be on to something," Abby replied in thought.

"I've got it!" Phil exclaimed, clicking his fingers. "Wasn't Lloyd the name of Edward Jenkins's firstborn son who died searching for the treasure?"

"You're right!" Mr. Baker gasped. "I wonder if that's what Detective Mortimer was really referring to. Maybe we can research his life, or at least as much as is known about it."

"I've got an idea," Mrs. Baker said. "We could split up, and some of us do research at the library while the rest of us find a Lloyds bank and ask about storing valuables there."

"Excellent," Mr. Baker agreed. "We'll meet up back at the library."

They found a Lloyds TSB branch, and Mrs. Baker, Andy, and Tom hopped out the car.

"You could head straight for the library," Mrs. Baker assured her husband. "We'll ask for directions and walk there. It can't be too far away."

Mr. Baker turned the car around and drove back the way he'd come. He soon pulled up in a parking spot in the road, and then he, Phil, and Abby hurried into the library. It was less modern than the library in Hertfordshire, and a friendly lady greeted them at the book returns desk as they walked in.

"Good morning, Ma'am, do you have a computer here that I could use?" Phil asked. His phone's battery had died in the car.

"Yes, certainly."

"I'm not a member of this library; is that a problem?"

"No. I can unlock one for you, and you may use it for an hour."

"Thank you."

"I'd like to use a computer too, if that's okay," Mr. Baker said to the librarian.

"That's fine; just follow me, please."

While the librarian led them to the computers, Abby looked for books on local history, and then scoured the books she found for any traces of information about Lloyd Jenkins.

As soon as Phil could, he e-mailed Detective Mortimer to update him on the latest news. Mr. Baker, in the meanwhile, used the internet for research on Lloyd Jenkins.

"Look here," Mr. Baker said excitedly after a quarter of an hour of searching. Phil leaned over to see his father's computer screen. "This is a website I found, and it has an extensive assortment of pieces about tragic deaths in the area, from the 1400s all the way through to today. I typed 'Lloyd Jenkins' in the search box, and look what's come up!

"It reads, 'Lloyd Jenkins was a merchant's son who came to Lizard in 1739. He expressed a desire to search the ocean floor for his father's treasure. His venture was mocked as impossible and foolish, but he could not be dissuaded. He hired a rowing boat one bright morning, and rowed on the calm sea all the way out to the reefs, according to one report. About midday, an unexpected squall blew up, and neither Lloyd nor the boat were ever seen again. Most likely they are both at the bottom of the ocean.'"

"Wow," Phil breathed. "What an amazing record."

"And that's not all. Just listen to this. 'Some of the villagers let their imaginations run wild, and they decided that they would see for themselves if the treasure really was down amongst the reefs. Several trips were made, and several strong fishermen dived down to explore the area, but no treasure was ever found.'"

"So the treasure was missing . . . already then!" Phil said, his jaw slack. "I wonder if it was never there."

"Well, at least we know that Marge wasn't confused about the Jenkins family history. Here is real evidence to back it up. Even Lloyd Jenkins believed there was a treasure. Unfortunately, he was wrong."

Phil frowned in thought. "Surely Edward Jenkins wasn't lying about having a treasure in the first place—or do you think he might have been?"

"I don't think he would have let his son risk his life in searching for a treasure that didn't even exist. I rather think that when Lloyd went after it, he was too late and somebody else had already found it."

"It's tragic that he lost his life looking for treasure that wasn't there," Phil breathed. "Maybe I should summarize that biography and send it to Detective Mortimer. I'm sure he'd like to know what we discover about Lloyd."

"Good idea," Mr. Baker nodded. "Remember to conceal it in code. I'll leave my browser window open so you can read the story. I'm going to find Abby."

He found her at a table scattered with open books. She was bent over the book nearest her, studying it meticulously.

"Have you found anything?" Mr. Baker asked, pulling up the other chair at the table.

"Nope, not really," she answered, "but I did make a copy of this map. It shows the outline of the coast very clearly, and it has a lot of detail. There's the infamous Manacles reef," she said, pointing to a region off the coast to the northeast of Lizard.

"That was very thoughtful of you," Mr. Baker paused and lowered his voice, "but the treasure is long gone."

"Long gone? Really?"

Mr. Baker nodded discreetly. "When Lloyd Jenkins went to find it, it wasn't there."

"It wasn't? How do we know?"

"I found an article about him on the Internet. Somebody must have found it before him."

Abby sighed and rested her head on her hands. "So we have no idea who took it, and no idea where to look?"

"I'm afraid so."

Mr. Baker helped Abby put the books away, and then they both went back to the computers, where Phil was typing furiously.

"There!" he said. "I've just finished sending the summary to Detective Mortimer in 'Aigy Paigy.' I must admit, I'm really getting the hang of it."

"Oh look, there's your mother and brothers," Mr. Baker said, noticing them walking towards the computers. "How did it go?" he asked when they came closer.

"It was fine," Mrs. Baker replied, "but I think that's the wrong lead."

"What I don't get," Andy frowned, "is how Edward's treasure could have ended up in a bank unless it was deposited hundreds of years ago."

"The bank would have to be hundreds of years old," Abby said sensibly.

Just then, Phil stiffened in his seat. "Don't look now, but the divers have arrived."

All the Bakers tensed up and cast a few furtive looks toward the library entrance.

"Okay, it's time to go," Mr. Baker said in a whisper, trying to sound calm but huskiness creeping into his voice.

Phil quickly logged off the computer and followed the others as they headed toward the entrance, passing the three divers as they did so. Abby tried not to look at them, fearing that doing so would give away the recognition in her eyes.

As they passed the lady at the book returns desk, she asked, "Have you finished on the computers?"

Phil, as he turned around to reply, noticed that the divers were already pulling up chairs for themselves at the computers. "Yes, thank you Ma'a –" he began before the words caught in his throat. His palms became sweaty, and he began twitching with heated anxiety as he exited the library. As soon as the Bakers were outside, he took a great gulp of cool air and then burst, "Let's go! We have to go NOW!"

"What is it, Phil?" Mr. Baker turned in surprise.

"Father, you left your browser window open so I could copy down the story of Lloyd," Phil's words raced, stumbling over each other in their hurry. "Well, I closed my browser window but I forgot to close yours! The divers will have seen it by now!"

Mr. Baker's eyes widened, and he looked as if he had been winded. "All right, everybody. Get in the car!" he commanded urgently.

They all dashed inside the car as quickly as they could, their hearts thumping violently. Mr. Baker swerved the car into the road and put his foot firmly on the accelerator. Abby told herself not to look back, but couldn't resist the urge for more than a few moments. As she looked back at the library, it becoming ever smaller, she saw a man rush out of the entrance and stare after the car as it disappeared around a bend.

CHAPTER 12

Only when they got home did Mr. Baker finally slow down. He had also seen the man watch them from the library, and worried that they'd be followed. But after some time of dodging around bends and driving nowhere in particular, he felt certain that nobody was on their tail. That didn't stop him from racing home as fast as safety allowed.

They all tumbled out of the car, shaking with pent-up adrenalin. They marched very quickly into their cottage and locked the door behind them.

"I am so sorry for my mistake," Phil said sincerely. "I only realized it once we had passed reception—and by then the divers were already seating themselves at the computers."

"Anybody could have made that mistake," Mr. Baker said. "We're just going to have to work around it."

Phil nodded.

"Now we've done two things," Mr. Baker continued. "We've let the divers know that we're after the treasure, and we've let them know that Lloyd Jenkins is the next subject of research."

Mr. Baker started pacing up and down the room, the cogs of his mind turning. "We're going to have to think harder, find clues quicker, act more wisely, and do our best not to cross paths with those men again."

"So what exactly did they find out that they weren't meant to?" Mrs. Baker asked.

As comprehensively as he could, Mr. Baker told what he had found about Lloyd Jenkins's death. "Somebody must have got to the treasure before he did," Mr. Baker finished.

Mrs. Baker nodded in understanding.

"I know!" Abby exclaimed. "We could disguise ourselves so the divers don't recognize us."

Andy raised his eyebrows. "Abby, our accents stand out like . . . like snowmen in . . . Hawaii! No amount of makeup could disguise them!"

Abby laughed at the mental image. "I guess you're right, but I'm sure I could imitate a neat English accent." She licked her lips, straightened up, and said, "I do believe it's time for tea and scones."

"Indubitably, but I think fish and chips are more fitting for the time of day," Andy replied, a posh expression taking over his features.

The others chuckled.

"I'm afraid to inform you that we don't have either of those options on the menu today," Mrs. Baker said, skillfully slipping into the accent of her childhood, "but I don't expect that anyone will mind too much if I pop ready-made lasagna into the oven."

"On the contrary dear, that sounds delightful," Mr. Baker replied. Then, as Mrs. Baker went to the kitchen area, he said, back in his American accent, "We'd better tell Detective Mortimer what happened."

Phil nodded, and quickly opened his laptop. In a few minutes, he had written a message and sent it.

"I wonder who would have found the treasure before Lloyd did," Abby thought aloud.

"I was just pondering the same thing," Mr. Baker said.

"Do you think the pirates who captured Edward Jenkins might've seen him drop his chest overboard?" Abby asked.

"If they had, wouldn't they have tried to retrieve it as soon as they could?"

Phil countered. "I mean, why wait?"

"What do you mean, Phil?" Mr. Baker asked.

"Well, the pirates had a battle with Edward's ship," Phil explained. "Once Edward was badly wounded, his crew surrendered. If the pirates had seen Edward drop something overboard, wouldn't they have wanted to look for it at that point?"

"But remember," Mr. Baker countered, "the sun would be rising, and the pirates would've wanted to get away as quickly as they could—before they were caught."

"Yes," Abby nodded. "They could've come back a few days later to search for the chest, disguised as merchants, and if they had found it, nobody would know."

"Edward Jenkins would know," Phil replied. "Remember, he was kept by the pirates until his ransom was paid. If they had found his treasure before then, I'm sure they would have taunted him about it."

"You're probably right," Mr. Baker said thoughtfully. "If it wasn't found by the pirates, and it wasn't found by Lloyd, it could have been found by *anybody* in-between." He breathed out heavily. "I wonder if this treasure-hunt is turning into a wild goose chase, after all."

"Didn't Detective Mortimer say that hired men were also looking for the treasure?" Mrs. Baker asked, walking towards them from the kitchen area.

"Yes, of course, Dear," Mr. Baker said, not sure what she meant. "We've concluded that the divers are those men, remember?"

"That's not what I mean," she shook her head, drying her hands on a dish-towel over her shoulder. "What I mean is this: Whoever hired those men believes the treasure is still out there somewhere. Maybe he has some inside information that we don't have. After all, he must be pretty determined to find the treasure if he's hired thugs to do it for him."

"You have a point," Mr. Baker said, his eyebrows raised at the new thought. "I wonder who their employer is."

"Oh," Phil muttered as a new e-mail appeared in his inbox. "I've got a message from the detective! And he's sent a set of numbers. '49.711161, -5.70488.' Now what is that?"

"It sounds like latitude and longitude coordinates," Mr. Baker said. He picked up his laptop and sat down on the couch. Just a few minutes later, he said, "It's an island about thirty miles south-west of where we are now."

Abby jumped up and started rummaging in her shoulder-bag, finally pulling out a piece of paper. "Here's the map I photocopied at the library—it cost only a few cents."

"Not cents," Andy corrected, "but pence."

"I wonder if the island is on here," Abby continued. She and Andy started searching the map for it.

"Why would Detective Mortimer give us that as a clue?" Mrs. Baker asked. "Does he want us to go there?"

"Maybe that's where the treasure is!" Abby exclaimed excitedly.

"Yes!" Phil nodded. "Maybe that's where it was put after somebody found it."

"Where does Detective Mortimer get all this information from, anyway?" Andy asked, a hint of admiration in his voice.

"Should I ask the detective if he means for us to go to that island?" Phil asked.

"Yes," Mr. Baker nodded.

Phil quickly coded a message to the detective, and a few minutes later received a reply. "He says that we must go there. That's all—he doesn't give any explanation for it."

"All right," Mr. Baker nodded. "The island it is then."

"How will we get there?" Mrs. Baker asked.

"Maybe we can hire a boat for the afternoon," Mr. Baker replied. He quickly did some research before concluding that hiring a boat was the best way to get to the island. He phoned a harbor with boats for hire, and the man suggested they come over to see them.

Bringing a backpack full of snacks, the Bakers headed back into their car. Mr. Baker had written down the postcode of the harbor and put it into the SatNav.

The drive to the harbor seemed long because of the excitement and urgency the Bakers were all feeling. They tried to concentrate on the old town they were passing through, and Andy continually snapped photos through the car's windows.

Finally, they pulled up outside an old building near the sea. Boats of all descriptions were lined up in the shallow harbor. Mr. Baker went inside the building and soon emerged beside a rather short man. They walked down to look at the boats, and the other Bakers followed.

The skipper was shriveled and bent with age and hard work. He wore an old, dark grey cap on his head, beneath which a pair of overgrown, grayish eyebrows peeked out. He had a wrinkled face, small eyes that had been narrowed to slits over years of squinting in bright sunlight, and a prominent nose. A pipe stuck out the corner of his thin mouth, and his hands were buried deep in his pockets as he discussed the boats with Mr. Baker.

"So you're heading out to sea, eh? To an island?" he asked. His eyes glanced curiously at the Bakers. "I must say, it's a very pleasant thing to do, though not a usual tourist activity." He chuckled, his pipe still between his teeth.

"No, it isn't," Mr. Baker replied, "but a friend recommended that we explore a particular island. I think it will be an exciting outing for my family and me."

"Certainly," the man nodded with a smile. "Well, when are you planning to head out?"

"As soon as we can," Mr. Baker said. "We don't have much time before we have to go back to America," he explained quickly, hoping not to give anything away.

"Hmm." The man looked out to sea with a thoughtful expression.

"We had actually been hoping to go this afternoon," Mr. Baker added.

"This afternoon?" the skipper turned incredulously. "Why, are you planning to camp overnight?"

"Er, no," Mr. Baker replied.

"If we leave now, we'd spend a lot of our time on the water, and only have about an hour on the island before having to head back. I don't want to be out at sea after darkness falls."

"Oh, I quite understand. I didn't realize we would need so much time to get there," Mr. Baker said.

"I'll tell you what," the man said. "You come here tomorrow morning—early—and we'll head out as soon as it's light enough. Then we can spend the better part of the day out on the island."

"That sounds great," Mr. Baker smiled. "What will we need to bring?"

"Bring plenty of food and water, wear sensible clothes, and don't forget sun lotion if you're prone to burning," and he motioned with a chuckle towards the sun. "If the weather's good tomorrow, which I think it will be, you'd better be ready for it." Then he looked at Andy with a grin. "And don't forget your camera. There's sure to be great scenery to capture."

Andy nodded. "I won't forget it."

"Thank you so much for your help," Mr. Baker said gratefully, shaking the man's hand. "We'll see you tomorrow then, Mr.—I'm sorry but I've forgotten your name, Mr. ...?"

"Mr. Alec Gimsby's my name," the man answered with a nod. "I'll have the boat ready when you come."

The Bakers left the harbor and got into their car, driving back to their holiday home and eating their snacks on the way.

"Is Mr. Gimsby coming with us?" Abby asked as they traveled.

"Yes," Mr. Baker nodded. "He's going to be the captain of our boat tomorrow."

"Why?" Tom asked.

"Even though I'm able to control a boat, I don't know enough about this coast to take us safely all the way to the island and back."

CHAPTER 13

The next morning, the Bakers followed Mr. Gimsby's advice, waking up bright and early, packing food and water, bringing sun lotion, and dressing sensibly. After family prayers for protection, they began the drive to the harbor.

"Phil," Abby said, "was there a new message from Detective Mortimer this morning?"

"No," Phil answered. "Last night I told him in an e-mail that we were heading out to the island today, and in his reply he said he was pleased to hear it. He hasn't written anything since then."

"So he hasn't given us any further clues?" Abby asked.

Phil shook his head. "No. I guess we'll just have to see what we find."

"Maybe Detective Mortimer just wants us to snoop around," Andy suggested. "I mean, how would he know exactly what to look for?"

When they arrived at the harbor, Alec came out of the old building to meet them.

"Morning," he grinned. "I've got our boat ready for today." Then, observing the backpacks the Bakers had brought, he said "I see you took my advice on clothing and food," and nodded approvingly. "Well come along."

He went down to the water's edge and then walked for a while before stopping at a rather clean, white motorboat tied up to the quay. He stepped inside the vessel and stowed away the backpacks he was handed.

"The *Opportunity*," Abby said softly as she read the name on the side of the boat. "Interesting name choice."

When they had boarded and were seated inside the cabin, Alec said, "Now, I'm sure you're sensible folks, but as a matter of course I've got to mention some rules. Keep your life jackets on at all times, and if you go out of the cabin, please don't dangle your arms and legs over the side of the boat." Then he started the motor and began navigating his way out the harbor.

There were many controls inside the boat, and the boys watched in fascination as Alec explained various ones. After a while, everybody went to the windows to soak up the beautiful morning views on the sea. Andy was very handy with his camera, taking shots of the sun still low in the sky, of his family members, and of the cliffs and the coastline that was becoming gradually more distant.

The Bakers were very grateful to be inside the cabin, sheltered from the cold and bracing sea air as it whipped past the boat.

After a good hour-and-a-half, the Bakers could see that they were nearing a group of rocks sticking out of the water. Alec steered skillfully around them, avoiding the rough waves that slapped against them and sent spray into the air.

Coming around the group of rocks, they saw a collection of little, black islands clustered in the shape of a half-moon, with one large, vegetated island in the middle. As Alec steered toward the largest island, Abby realized they were entering a natural bay that was somewhat sheltered from the waves.

Alec spotted a good landing area and steered toward it, slowing down as he approached. Finally, he drove the boat right onto the sand of the island's beach. Everybody got out of the boat, and Mr. Baker and the boys helped Alec pull it up as high as they could, securing it to a large rock.

"Well, we're here," Alec said, straightening up. "I'll wait by the boat. If the weather changes and we need to leave, I'll find you."

The Bakers climbed up the beach and paused to survey their beautiful surroundings. There were jagged rocks along the shoreline, except for the place where the boat had landed. There, the rocks gave way to a stretch of beach, which ended abruptly at a brown cliff face. Straw-colored grass, which quivered at every breath of sea breeze, peeked over the low cliffs. At the top of the island, the Bakers could just see the tops of some trees.

They started walking toward the cliff face, and then searched for a way up it. Phil found a part of the cliff that had given way to a slope, and with the help of tufts of grass, he and Andy clambered up it quickly, followed by Mr. and Mrs. Baker, Abby, and Tom. From there they had a better view of the surrounding sea and the top of the island.

They walked in the direction of the few trees they could see, Andy documenting almost every step with photos. They clambered over rough areas and strolled pleasantly along smooth, grassy stretches.

The place was apparently a haven for Great Black-backed and Yellow-legged gulls, because there were many around. As the Bakers ventured further into the island, great clouds of them fluttered up from the ground, calling in surprise to one another.

Gradually, the scenery changed. Plants and flowers flourished, and leafy trees blocked out the light as the party entered a wooded area. Abby shivered. Without the sunlight, the air was quite cool.

"Isn't this beautiful?" Mrs. Baker whispered. Somehow, whispering seemed fitting in the dense forest. The only other sounds were the rustle of leaves in the breeze and the waves washing over rocks on the coast.

They came into a clearing and stopped for a rest, when Andy asked, "Are those markings on that tree there?" He jumped forward to have a closer look. "Yes, they are markings! Made with a knife, I'm sure!"

The others came over to see for themselves and were very surprised to see tally marks on the tree.

"They look very old," Mr. Baker said.

"Maybe they were done by an ancient castaway!" Andy exclaimed.

"A castaway?!" Abby repeated, her pulse quickening. "Do you really think so?"

"Well," Mr. Baker said, "I imagine this is a precarious place for ships, particularly at night."

"At night!" Abby cried, her eyes shining. "And in a storm! A ship could easily run aground on the rocks we passed, and it's likely there were pirates around here. Maybe we should go diving around here and see what we can find."

"This doesn't seem right," Phil said. "Edward Jenkins's map obviously led to the coast off Lizard Point. Why would he lead somebody there, his own son included, if he was really shipwrecked here? Surely he wasn't that disoriented—I mean, this is miles away from Lizard."

"Maybe that wasn't his map," Andy suggested. "Maybe his got confused with somebody else's."

Phil frowned. "Remember, the article Father found said that Lloyd was searching off the Lizard peninsula. Obviously the map led him there."

"Edward must have been so disoriented that he unwittingly led his son to the wrong place. And that means," Abby said, snapping her fingers, "that nobody removed the treasure from the Lizard after all! It was never there in the first place!"

"Exactly!" Andy joined.

"Well," Mr. Baker said, "let's carry on walking and see what we find."

The wooded area thinned out a little, and the Bakers kept their eyes peeled for clues of past human activity. They had gone only a little further when Andy gasped and pointed to a cave entrance in a nearby rock wall.

"A cave!" Abby exclaimed.

"Let's explore it!" Andy said excitedly.

Mr. Baker led the way to the cave, slowing down as he approached it. Fortunately the entrance was wide enough to let a decent amount of light in, and Mr. Baker stepped inside. Phil and Andy were just behind him.

The cave was rather small, and the roof quite low. On the left side were scattered crude stone and wooden tools. A bit further inside were carved, wooden bowls, and on floor to the right, peeking out from beneath tattered clothes, were the bones of a skeleton.

Shivers ran up the spines of the three people in the cave, and they soon left it.

"What's it like in there?" Abby asked eagerly.

Andy, looking a little pale answered, "Oh, somebody lived here all right. Lived—and died."

"A skeleton?" Mrs. Baker asked quickly.

Mr. Baker nodded.

"Who do you think it was?" Abby asked.

"We have no idea," Phil said, shaking his head.

"Father, could I please go inside?" she asked.

"All right," Mr. Baker said. "You can come with me."

They both stepped inside the cave. The silence was eerie, and as soon as Abby saw the skeleton, she felt sick in the pit of her stomach.

"I'm . . . heading out," she whispered quickly.

Mr. Baker nodded understandingly and started walking towards the entrance when something on the floor beside the skeleton caught his eye. He knelt down and looked closely before finally reaching out his hand and picking up the piece of worn leather. Beneath it were two leather-bound books that looked very, very old.

He stepped outside, into the brighter light, to examine the books. The others crowded around as soon as they caught sight of what Mr. Baker was holding.

"This is an old Bible," Mr. Baker said in surprise as he opened the larger of the two books. "This one seems to be a diary." He almost gasped in surprise as his eyes traveled down the first page. "Listen ! 'This is the diary of Lloyd John Jenkins, son of Edward John Jenkins, manager of Bracken Estate,'" Mr. Baker paused as surprised gasps and remarks came from all the members of his family. When they recovered from their surprise, he continued.

"The first entry reads,

'2 September, 1739. Father gave me this diary, identical to his own ones, only a month ago—before I told him anything of my plan to search for the possessions he lost in a shipwreck some years ago. Before I set out on this errand, I had not the time nor inclination to write, but now I believe I have both.

143

'Lord willing, I will pen the miserable tale of how I happen to be here. It is miserable because I fear I will never be rescued, and will have to live out my days in this lonely place. Verily, I have learnt the value of all I used to possess—friends, family, and a comfortable home. Indeed, now that I look back on what once discontented me, I realize that I have made a very foolish trade. It cannot rightly be called a trade, however, for my destiny was not entirely in my hands. Had it been, I would have returned safely home with a large inheritance to my name. I fear that never will be the case.

'I travel back in time to August 15, when I left my loving parents, brothers, and friends to embark on the daring mission to recover my father's wealth. The trip from Hertfordshire to Cornwall took over a week, so that I only arrived near Lizard on the 28th.

'I was determined to go out to the reefs, the dreaded rocks upon which many a ship has been lost, the very next day. The local people tried to dissuade me when they heard my mission, calling it a fool's errand, but I did not heed their warnings. I have regretted my arrogant presumption ever since.

'No man would sail out with me, believing the weather too unpredictable, and finally, only by offering a large sum of money, did I hire a rowing boat from a fisherman and set out immediately that bright morning.

'I rowed right to the place specified on the map my good father made, and, being a strong swimmer, dived into the water. I reached the shallow bottom fairly easily and succeeded in locating the chest within my first few dives. I secured a rope to the chest, whereupon I re-entered the rowing boat and endeavoured to pull the chest up to the surface, using the side of the boat as leverage. It was difficult and tiresome work, and by the time the heavy chest was safely aboard, I scarcely had strength left in me to row back to shore. Indeed, a strong wind had already blown up, and the waves were growing choppy and restless.

'I determined to reach the shore before the storm, which was inevitably coming, and thereby prove to the villagers that their fears on my behalf had been unfounded, such a strong and invincible youth was I. That was not to be so. I had rowed barely a quarter of the way back when my arms gave out and could no longer battle the current, which was growing stronger every minute. The waves grew fiercer and more unruly, until they formed enormous mounds over which my poor, little boat was obliged to climb. That little vessel pitched and rolled so violently that more than once I felt certain I would be tossed into the raging water. I was sure the end of my life was nigh. Without the chest to stabilize it somewhat, I believe the boat would have capsized very quickly.

'The tempest raged for longer than I care to remember. It seemed to last for hours, and the sky became so dark that I am persuaded it lasted throughout the night. In my exhausted state, I believe I slipped out of consciousness once or twice, only to be roused by a drenching of frigid seawater washing over the side of the boat.

'The storm so terrified me that my prayers became very fervent indeed. I vowed the Lord that if He brought me to safety, I would endeavour to do away with greed and pride entirely, even to the point of abandoning the treasure that would fall to me upon my father's death.

'It was in the early hours of the morning that the end of my nightmarish experience came. Tossed about by the waves, the boat was heading directly for a dark outline on the water, which appeared to be jagged rocks. Terror filled me as, try as I might, I was unable to steer the boat and it was thrown mercilessly onto the rocks. The impact was so great that I was cast head-first into the foaming water. It is a mercy I was tossed clear of the rocks, for if I had not been, this account would not exist. Staying afloat was the most I could do in the boisterous waves, until I was certain I could no longer do even that. A great wave picked me up and slammed me directly on this beach. When the wave receded, I was left winded and gasping for air like a landed fish.

'I knew I had to get up to higher ground to escape the rough sea, and by the grace of God, I was able to drag myself up a grassy incline beyond the reach of the waves. There I finally collapsed, falling deep into unconsciousness.

'I awoke, later that morning or perhaps the next, I know not which, with the sun beating down mercilessly upon me. My muscles ached, my throat burned from all the salt-water I had swallowed, and my head throbbed beyond description. I could not will myself to move, and yet I knew that I would die of dehydration and perhaps sunstroke if I did not.

'I opened my eyes slowly, blinking frequently, but the bright sunshine sent a piercing pain to my head. I closed my eyes and rested a few minutes more on the sand before trying to open them again. I lifted my head up with difficulty, and eased myself onto my hands and knees, in which position I was able to drag myself a few feet higher up the slope and onto more grass. I was then obliged to rest again. In this manner I moved myself all the way up the slope and into the shade of a nearby bush. The distance was not more than forty feet, and yet it took severe determination to travel that far in my condition. My mouth was parched and dry, and I desperately longed for a drink, yet I could not move any further, nor did I know if there was any fresh water to be found on the island.

'I lapsed in and out of consciousness throughout that day, so dehydrated and battered by the storm was I. The thought of possible death crossed my mind a few times in my stupor, and I believe I endeavoured to pray, though I could not get beyond a few words which I cannot now bring to mind.

'It must have been in the evening that I was awoken by a gentle pattering sound, and by the uncomfortable feeling of being cold and wet. My mind took a while to realize what was happening, but when it finally did, my heart fairly leapt with joy. Rain was falling from the sky, making my survival more of a possibility than it had yet been. I turned upon my back and opened my parched mouth to catch some of the life-preserving drops, and when I recovered enough to feel the full extent of my thirst, I slowly pulled myself to a sitting position and began lapping water from a nearby puddle.

'My faculties returned to me, and I realized that the rain was a merciful blessing from the Lord, whereupon I determined to collect as much of it as I could. Having no vessel in which to catch it, however, I was at a loss for what to do. I stood up and searched for something to use. Happening to glance toward the shoreline, I saw a rounded, wooden object snagged on some rocks. I was to learn that it was a remnant from the poor boat I had hired. I managed to salvage the object, which was the prow of the boat, and set it up in such a way as to trap some rainwater.

'I have been living on this island ever since then, three days, and am slowly growing accustomed to island survival, even making myself some rough tools from rock and wood.

'Upon following a faintly trickling stream on the day after the rain, I discovered, to my immense relief, a small freshwater lake in the middle of the island. Upon washing my face in the water, I discovered a bloodstained, painful gash and swelling on one side of my head, undoubtedly the cause of my severe headache the previous day. It continues to cause me a deal of pain, but I have done all I can to help it heal.

'The lake has been my faithful supply of water these few days, as the Brook Cherith was to the prophet Elijah, and I believe it will continue to be so.'"

Mr. Baker paused in his reading as he came to the end of the entry, and he looked up at the faces around him. "Isn't it a mercy that Lloyd survived the storm?" he commented in awe.

"Oh, yes!" the answer came from all directions.

"That's a valuable piece of history," Mrs. Baker said with an impressed nod toward the diary.

"A better tale I've never heard, except in fiction," Abby said.

"Does he mention the treasure again?" Mrs. Baker asked.

"Let's hope he does," Andy said.

"We'll have to continue to find out," Mr. Baker nodded.

"Can we sit down somewhere?" Mrs. Baker asked. "I'm getting tired of standing."

"And hungry!" Tom added.

"Maybe we can set out our picnic blankets and have a few snacks," Andy suggested.

Everybody seemed to like that idea, so the Bakers headed back to the clearing in the wood. Mr. Baker and Phil flapped the picnic blankets and laid them out on the ground. As soon as they were down, Mrs. Baker, the twins, and Tom started laying out the snacks.

Soon they were ready for Mr. Baker to resume his reading, which he eagerly did.

"Here's the next entry," he said.

"'14 September, 1739. In the days after landing on the island, I determined to find my father's treasure once more. I was unable to venture underwater, though the sea was calm and inviting, for the salty water stung my wounded head very badly. I instead explored the numerous rock pools around the island and collected seaweed for my food, also catching the abounding crabs and snails I found as my means of combating starvation. I do not exaggerate when I say that I was merely combating starvation, for that form of food is not to my liking.

'In my foraging expeditions, I have frequently discovered pieces of broken wood. The pieces range in size from splinters all the way to large planks, and I recognize them all as the remainders of my hired boat. Though I did not expect the boat to have survived the fury of the waves and impact upon the rocks in the storm, seeing it so dismembered is a great disappointment, as it would have meant a possible return to civilization. I have promised the Lord that if He sees fit to ever return me there, I will handsomely repay the fisherman for the damages to his boat.

'Growing tired of the crab meat and snail flesh, I spent much time learning to catch the little fish stranded in the rock pools by receding tides. They have been a welcome addition to my staple diet, however small that addition happens to be. Failing that, my thoughts turn to the numerous gulls on the island, and I have devised many schemes in order to catch them. Thus far, all my plans on that note have failed.

'20 September, 1739. I have heretofore not mentioned the cave in which I have been living since I arrived on the island. It is of a reasonable size and I have done all I can to make it comfortable.

'The wound to my head has been healing well, thanks be to God, and I am able to venture underwater in my search for food and my father's treasure. The position of the rocks on either side of the island forms a bay, which is most convenient for swimming. Only in storms, it seems, are the rocks insufficient to calm the waves in the bay.

'I have been persuaded that the treasure would have sunk directly when it left the boat, and it therefore should be somewhere near the rocks the boat struck. Today, on my diving expedition, I discovered that my suspicion was correct. Swimming underwater in the area around the rocks, I caught sight of something glinting in the sunlight which streamed through the water. Upon taking a closer look, I found the treasure chest, my rope still attached to it, concealed beneath some seaweed.

'I rose to the surface for a breath, and then dived down again, taking hold of the rope and tugging at it with all my might. The chest would not budge, and I finally decided to leave it there. I do not expect it to move in my absence, and I am satisfied with the knowledge of where it is. My former self would not have rested until the chest was safely in my possession, but after all that has transpired, I am not half as greedy as I was. The Lord has certainly aided me in overcoming that vile flaw, and my prayer is that He help my four brothers to do the same.

'I have set up a calendar in the back of this book, so that I do not lose track of time or of the days of the week. It would be a tragedy, indeed, to forget Sundays, upon which I devote myself to especial prayer and meditation upon the words of Scripture I have in my memory.

'My only complaint is my lack of a Bible, which I sorely feel. How grateful I am now for all the Scriptures I memorized in my youth! I repeat them often to myself, and strain to remember every word of fleeting passages I occasionally recall.

'23 September, 1739. Today I caught my first fish upon a spear I fashioned from island materials. Fishing in this way has taken a great deal of patience, and a great number of failures, to learn. The warm, calm bay teems with fish, yet thus far they have been of no benefit to me save in targets to aim at. Even in this victory, I realize it will be a long time before I am able to catch fish in this manner with any degree of constancy.

'In the back of my mind, I have a nagging anxiety that winter will soon be upon the island, and I am not in the least prepared for its arrival. The weather I have experienced in these last few weeks persuades me that the climate is milder here than at home; however I would like to be prepared for whatever comes my way.

'Another thought that frequently crosses my mind is that in winter, I may be unable to swim in the sea without catching a chill. For this reason, then, and with the Lord's blessing, I will endeavour to once more retrieve my father's treasure, this time coming upon land and using my full, recovered strength to hoist it up. I plan also to catch as many fish as I possibly can, and to smoke them for storage throughout the colder months. The gulls, I believe, will then become my staple diet, with fish being supplements to it.

'Since I am unacquainted with the plants that grow on the island, I consider it prudent to refrain from eating them. I have consumed only seaweed these long weeks, and the thought of a juicy apple or a crisp lettuce fairly makes my mouth water.

'The island fruits do have their uses, however. The ink I am using at this moment is made from the juice of small, crimson berries.

'I still pray daily for rescue from this island, though my prayers now turn more towards the welfare of my family members and friends. I believe the Lord is making me more content with a secluded life. It is not lonely, for He is ever with me, and I am grateful to be closer to Him than I ever have been. In my prayers I often catch myself referring to the island as my own, and I would very much like to name it, seeing as I do not know its proper name.

'26 September, 1739. I recovered my father's chest on the 24th, and it has rested in my shelter since then. I greatly desire to pry it open, but I cannot make up my mind whether or not this is a temptation I ought to resist.

'The chest belongs to my father, and that being the case, I do not wish to give myself the liberty of taking possession of that which does not belong to me, however right my future inheritance may be. However, items may be in the chest which would be of invaluable use to me, and, further, I ought to make certain that the chest I discovered is indeed my father's.

'I do not have the key to the chest, as my father did not give it to me, but I have already struck upon the easiest way to pry the chest open while causing it the least damage possible.

'27 September, 1739. I finally decided to open the chest, and am intensely grateful that I did. The chest is indeed my father's, for I found his fortune of gold coins.

'However, by far the most valuable thing the chest contains is an old volume, wrapped securely in calf leather, which I was enraptured to discover is my father's Bible. The gold means nothing on this island, but the Bible is a treasure that is most precious to me.

'Since the Bible is the only thing of use, and since I would not want the treasure to be found if anyone chances to land here, I have decided to hide it as best I can.

'2 October, 1739. The chest is hidden, and I feel somehow able to rest easier now that it is so.

'The weather is certainly milder and more pleasant here than at home, but the sea does have a penchant for becoming violent and casting spray far onto the island.

'In whiling away these colder months, I struck upon the idea of leaving riddles directing to the location of the chest. I would not have anyone mistakenly think that I consider wealth an evil thing. On the contrary, wealth used for righteous purposes is a great boon indeed, and I hope that if the treasure ever is found, it will be used as God intends—in aid of the poor, needy, orphaned, or widowed,'" Mr. Baker paused with his eyebrows raised in surprise, " 'or for any other righteous action.

'I intend to riddle the clues to the treasure to ensure, to some degree, that only those who would use it rightly will find it.'"

Mr. Baker broke off suddenly and looked up from the book. Andy was tapping his arm urgently, and Mr. Baker looked at his son with a questioning look.

"Father, listen to that! Can you hear? It's a motorboat!"

The others had been concentrating so hard on the story that they hadn't noticed the faint whirr of an engine over the surrounding sounds. They all listened intently.

"A motorboat!" Mr. Baker cried. "I wonder if it's Alec?"

Mr. Baker, Phil, and Andy stood up and went back the way they had come, stopping at the edge of the wooded area to look out to sea. There, nearing the beach, was a white motorboat. Three men were inside it.

CHAPTER 14

"The divers!" Phil muttered in horror.

Andy snapped a photo, wearing a grim expression on his face.

"They will have seen our boat by now," Phil continued.

"We must stay hidden for at least as long as we can," Mr. Baker said in an urgent tone, leading the way back to the others in silence, wondering what could be done.

"We've got company," Mr. Baker announced as he approached the rest of his family. "It's the divers."

"Oh, no," Mrs. Baker groaned. Abby's eyes widened.

"Maybe we could head to the other side of the island and swim back to our boat without them seeing us," Phil suggested. "We could get away."

"They'd find the treasure!" Abby gasped.

"Not without Lloyd's diary," Phil replied.

"They won't leave the boats unguarded," Mr. Baker pointed out grimly. "They'll be expecting us to try to give them the slip."

"Trees," Andy said. "We could climb trees and be hidden until help arrives."

"Help isn't arriving," Phil muttered, his eyes glued to the screen of his Smartphone. "I can't pick up a signal out here."

"Neither can I," Mr. Baker said, checking his own mobile. "The divers know that *somebody's* here," he paused, "and Alec won't think of pretending to have come alone. Since they'll know we're here, there's no point in hiding. Our best chance is to try the 'tourist family' pose, and hope our little encounter with them at the library went over their heads."

He began emptying one of the backpacks and set out the juices and plastic cups. Mrs. Baker, the twins, and Tom caught on, and started unpacking the knives and forks.

"Here's your juice, Tom," Andy said, putting a plastic cup in his little brother's hand before dashing to the next person.

"I didn't want orange juice," Tom complained. "I asked for apple juice, remember?"

"Hush, Tom," Mrs. Baker whispered. "Now's not the time to be picky."

"Sit down, everybody," Mr. Baker instructed, "and let's say grace."

They all sat down and bowed their heads for the most unusual grace they had ever heard.

"Lord, thank you for your providing this food. Please help us to be calm, and whatever happens, keep us safe in Your hands. In Jesus' name, amen."

Everybody added an 'amen' and then looked at the food on the blankets. Abby put a helping of salad on her plate and popped a tomato into her mouth, but her stomach felt like it was twisting into a knot, and she could hardly force herself to swallow. She looked at the faces around her and decided that the others felt the same way.

Andy's cheeks were flushed pink as he munched determinedly on a hamburger. Mrs. Baker's face was pinched and pale, and all she could manage to do was sip the orange juice Tom didn't want. Tom stood up and looked in the direction of the beach until he was told to sit down again. Phil stared fixedly at the center of the blanket as he chewed, his ears straining to catch the faintest sound in the distance. Mr. Baker had imposed a tranquil expression on his face, though Abby could see lines of worry around his eyes.

Phil reached for the packet of crisps, giving Abby a reassuring look as he did so. Only then did she realize how nervous she probably looked, and quickly took a bite of hamburger to hide it.

Mrs. Baker was picking at some salad and Andy was just finishing his burger when the sound of breaking sticks and crunching leaves grew loud.

"We know you're here," a rough voice called, "and no matter where you are, we'll find you sooner or later!"

Just then, one of the three divers walked into the clearing with one of his accomplices just behind him. Alec was being prodded along from behind. The diver in front, evidently the one who had called out, stopped in surprise when he saw the Bakers sitting on blankets having a picnic.

"Uh, excuse me?" Mr. Baker asked, attempting to sound unaware of what was going on.

"So, we've caught you by surprise?" the man grinned, rubbing his chin. "Well, well, well!"

"What do you mean by that, Mr. ...?" Mr. Baker inquired, setting down his plate.

"Charles Baker, you can call me Rich."

"How do you know my name?" Mr. Baker spluttered.

"Our boss got hold of your son's correspondence with Detective Mortimer. From there, finding your details was easy. Actually, finding you was easy too."

"Yeah," one of the thugs called Martin sniggered. "We were already planning to come to this island when we found out that Detective Mortimer had sent you here too."

Rich nodded. "We know you're after the same treasure as us, and so we're going to have to stop you."

"Leave my wife and children out of this," Mr. Baker said sternly.

"No need to worry, Charlie," Rich laughed. "We don't intend to harm anyone. We'll probably leave you all stranded here; that's all."

"As I said, I'm not one of them," Alec said quickly. "I'm just the skipper they hired. I don't know what's going on."

"Well perhaps our friends here can enlighten us," Rich said, looking at the Bakers. "What do you know about the treasure?" he asked Phil.

"All we know is –" Mr. Baker began before he was rudely interrupted.

"I asked *him*," Rich thundered before turning back to Phil. "So?"

"Well," Phil began, "we're tourists who want to help a lady who has Alzheimer's Disease, and that's why we're looking for the treasure. It belongs to her."

"How sweet," Rich replied, his voice thick with sarcasm. "So where is the treasure?"

"I don't know," Phil shook his head. "We haven't been here long. You should've given us more time."

One of the divers chuckled, but Rich was serious. "I'm going to ask you again. Have you found out where the treasure is hidden? Is it on this island?"

Abby's heart thumped wildly every time Rich asked a question, and she almost sighed with relief every time Phil dodged one. She waited in suspense as Phil thought up an answer.

"I'm telling the truth when I say I don't know where it is. The only way to find out if it's on this island is to look," Phil said. "We would've started after lunch, but your arrival has interrupted our plans."

"All right," Rich nodded, "you and your family stay put. Martin, you stay here too and guard this lot. I'm going to fetch Billy and invite Charlie to come exploring with us." At first nobody knew who he was referring to, but then it became apparent that he wanted Mr. Baker to go with him.

"That's Mr. Baker to you, Richard, or whatever your name is," he replied soberly, rising to his feet and glancing at his family members. His eyes rested on Phil, and then he set his jaw in quiet confidence and followed Rich through the forest, back towards the beach.

Once they were well away, Martin said, "Hey, could you pass me a burger?"

Phil felt galled at the thought of feeding a thug, but then he remembered the text about refreshing hungry and thirsty enemies and held one out.

Martin grabbed the burger and sank his teeth into it. The others sat in tense silence, wondering where Mr. Baker was and how long they would remain prisoners on the picnic blanket.

"Good burger," Martin complimented as he took another large bite.

Abby quickly summed Martin up. He was a tall, heavyset man with a slightly bulging belly and a fleshy face. After a while, he seemed to grow tired of standing because he sat down and wiped his forehead. "You got something to drink?" he asked. The others exchanged glances.

"Um," Andy stammered, "we've got two types of juice: orange and apple. The apple isn't open yet."

"I'd like apple juice!" Tom burst.

Martin chuckled and licked his lips. "So would I."

Andy got up to fetch two plastic cups and poured apple juice into both of them. As Andy handed him the cup, Martin said a quick, "Thanks, and do you have any burgers left?"

Time passed slowly, and the Bakers and Alec remained rooted to the picnic blanket for what seemed like hours. Alec looked like the only comfortable one out of them all, with his hands clasped around his knees, his eyes closed, and his pipe puffing softly.

Martin was getting sleepy at his post against the tree, so he stood up, dusted himself off, and began pacing up and down, always keeping one eye fixed on his prisoners.

Eventually, Phil picked up the courage to clear his throat and ask, "How did you find your way here?"

"Well, after we saw you at the library, we realized that you were also after the Jenkins treasure. Our boss knew Detective Mortimer was working on the case, and he found out about your connection with him. I guess he hired someone to hack into your e-mail account so we could see all your correspondence with Detective Mortimer."

"But the messages were coded."

"Someone cracked the code," Martin shrugged. "Detective Mortimer had sent you the coordinates of this place, so we knew we'd kill two birds with one stone: a, catch you, and b, find the treasure."

Phil nodded slowly in understanding.

Alec opened one eye. "So Martin, what are you going to do with the treasure? Spend it on something nice?"

"Oh, I'll only get a small cut of it," Martin shrugged again. "Not sure what I'll do with it yet. Probably waste it," he chuckled.

The Bakers exchanged glances. "Martin, don't you realize that you're stealing from an elderly widow who needs the money to stay in her own home? Surely you don't want to have that on your conscience," Phil said.

Martin shifted uncomfortably. "I might not be a good person," he frowned, "but that doesn't mean I'm a bad person. I may even give some of the treasure money to charity."

Half an hour later, Rich, Mr. Baker, and Billy came back to the clearing. "Look what we got!" Rich cried triumphantly, waving two leather-bound books under Martin's nose. "Can you smell the treasure?"

"What?" Martin asked, confused.

"This book fell out of Charlie's pocket," Rich grinned, "and that naturally made us find the other one he had. One of them is the diary of Lloyd Jenkins, and it's got clues to the treasure inside it."

"The diary of who?" Martin asked.

"Lloyd Jenkins," Rich answered. "The eldest son of Edward Jenkins. It turns out he was stranded here, and buried the treasure on this island. We even found his cave and his skeleton. So now all we have to do is follow the clues, find the treasure, and go home rich men. Ha! I'll really be *Rich* then!" he snorted with laughter.

"Let's find this treasure before becoming too excited," Billy said in a fearsomely deep voice, breaking through Rich and Martin's laughter. "If we don't hurry up, we'll hear from the Boss about it. And then the *only* money you'll have is that in your name."

Rich's face became sullen.

"I want to see the clues too," Martin said quickly. "I've been on guard duty long enough."

"No Martin," Billy replied. "We all know you're no good at solving riddles."

"Riddles?" Martin frowned. "Who said anything about riddles?"

"The clues are hidden inside riddles," Rich explained.

"Why would anyone do something like that?" Martin complained.

"Lloyd hid the clues inside riddles so that *bad men* like us wouldn't be able to find the treasure," Rich chuckled.

"What are we going to do then?" Martin asked.

"*You're* going to stay here and guard while Billy and I solve the riddles in a nice, quiet spot." With that, he began walking away through the forest.

Martin sighed grumpily and folded his arms. "Why do I always get the boring jobs?" he muttered under his breath.

Mr. Baker sat down on the picnic blanket, and his family members were very relieved to see him. Mrs. Baker looked at him with sad eyes. "The diary," she mouthed.

Mr. Baker nodded disappointedly. A few minutes later, he bowed his head and shut his eyes, and the others could tell he was praying.

Lord, Abby prayed silently, *we have come so far to find the treasure, and now it seems it'll be stolen, and we'll be stranded here. Please protect us and use us to find the treasure so we can help Mrs. Fielding.*

It was half an hour later that Rich and Billy returned, sulky and annoyed.

"So, geniuses," Martin gloated, "where's this treasure? Already in the boat? Or were the riddles too lofty for you?"

"You stay out of this," Billy growled in a menacing tone.

"We're going to get our goody-two-shoes prisoners to solve the riddles for us," Rich mumbled.

Abby's eyebrows shot up. *Lord,* her prayer raced silently, *this isn't what I meant when I asked that we'd be <u>used</u> to find the treasure!*

"Riddle number one," Rich read in his rough accent. "The place called Cherith where the prophet Elijah received refreshment." He looked up at the Bakers as they exchanged glances. "It's in the Bible, isn't it?" he asked.

Martin laughed. "No wonder you couldn't get anywhere with riddles like that!"

"Keep quiet, Martin!" Rich threatened, keeping his eyes on the Bakers. "We have Lloyd's own Bible, so we could search the whole thing for the answers if only we had enough time. So what's the answer?" he asked the Bakers.

"Uh, remind us why we would help you," Mr. Baker replied in a questioning tone.

"Because we've got control over the only transport out of here," Rich answered.

"And we don't have consciences," Billy added menacingly.

Mr. Baker looked thoughtful.

"Come on, now," Rich said, resting his hand on his gun. "The place called Cherith where the prophet Elijah received refreshment."

"I know the answer," Martin said quickly. "It was a river or something."

Rich and Billy looked at Martin in surprise. "A river? Are you sure?"

"Of course I'm sure!"

"All right, everybody on your feet," Rich said. "We're going to that river."

"Wait," Mr. Baker said. "My family is staying here."

"Oh no, they aren't," Billy replied in a spine-chilling tone.

"Then let my wife and youngest child stay here," Mr. Baker said firmly. "Thomas would only slow us down, and he needs his mother to look after him."

Rich and Billy looked thoughtful for a few moments, and then Rich muttered, "Oh, all right then. It'll make no difference to us."

CHAPTER 15

The rest of them stood up, Alec included, and began trudging through the forest in the direction Rich was leading. Martin watched the side of the procession, and Billy brought up the rear, his hand resting threateningly on his Beretta.

They walked along until they came to a clearing, where grass and stinging nettles carpeted the ground in a downward slope. The slope ended in a shallow stream with pebbles scattered at the bottom. On the other side of the stream was a narrow bank, leading onto another steep slope covered in thorny and stinging plants.

"You found the river quickly, Rich," Martin commented.

"We passed it earlier," Rich nodded. "Now for our next riddle. 'As found in the book of Revelation, the place of fire and brimstone where the devil shall spend eternity.' Now surely the answer to that is Hell," he said, "but I don't see how that's a clue."

Martin raised an eyebrow. "Me neither. So, what's the real answer?" he asked, turning to the Bakers.

Mr. Baker looked thoughtfully at the stream. "A place of fire and brimstone...."

"Could that be," Phil paused, "the Lake of Fire?"

Mr. Baker only sighed. He had been hoping nobody would suggest that.

"Lake of Fire?" Martin questioned. "How's that a clue?"

"The clue must be lake," Rich answered. "So let's follow this brook upstream until we get to one."

Rich picked his way down the slope and then leaped across the stream to the narrow bank on the other side. "Come on," he called. "I want you all to cross."

They stepped carefully down the thorny slope and then tried to leap across the stream as Rich had done. Abby needed Mr. Baker to give her a hand, but soon everybody was across and once more following Rich.

At some places the narrow bank disappeared completely, and some of the Bakers found themselves sliding frighteningly down the muddy slope and grabbing onto thorny branches or stinging nettles to stop themselves. Rich was quite nimble over the tricky parts, but Martin struggled along.

Finally, they climbed up an incline and found themselves looking at a still lake bordered by trees, grass, and even some flowers. While they sat down for a breather, Rich read the next clue.

"I will lift my eyes unto these, from whence cometh my help," he said.

"The heavens?" Martin suggested, looking up at the sky.

Rich looked up too, a frown on his face. Then he looked back at Martin and shook his head.

"I can't think of what else they could be," Martin shrugged.

"Well, it's a good thing I wasn't asking you," Rich replied sharply. "I was asking our prisoners."

"Can't we just have a bit of a rest?" Abby asked, exaggerating her panting.

"No, you can't," Rich answered. "Look at the sky, as Martin so cleverly suggested. The sun will start setting soon, and I intend to have the treasure before then. There's no time to waste. What is the answer to my question?"

"Could you repeat the question?" Andy asked, trying to buy some time.

"I will lift up mine eyes unto these, from whence cometh my help," Rich repeated.

"That's easy," Abby blurted, and then she instantly wished she hadn't.

"Oh really? Do enlighten us," Rich said.

"Er," Abby hesitated, "I will lift up my eyes...to the...."

"Trees," Andy finished.

"The trees?" Martin raised an eyebrow. "That doesn't make any sense."

"Well," Andy said, "just think of the olden days when the most fearsome weapons that existed were bows and arrows. If you were running through the forest, being chased by your enemies, you would hope that one of your friends was up in a tree to shoot the people chasing you."

There was a thoughtful silence as Andy finished his explanation, and the thugs began looking up at the trees.

"So what are we supposed to find?" Rich asked.

"I suppose we're meant to find a very large or prominent tree," Phil suggested.

They all started walking around the lake, trying to spot a tree that matched Phil's description. When the thugs felt satisfied that they had found the largest, most prominent tree nearby, Rich read the next clue.

"Listen up," he said. "Jesus calmed the storm in the middle of this body of water," he said. "So where was He?"

"He fed the five thousand people on a grassy mountainside, didn't he?" Andy put in, hoping to lead the thugs onto the wrong track.

"What does that have to do with calming a storm?" Rich demanded.

"Er," Andy hesitated.

"The lake Jesus had to cross to get to the mountain where he fed the five thousand was a stormy one," Mr. Baker said, calculating every word before he said it.

"You're telling me that there were storms in the middle of a lake?" Rich asked in disbelief, glancing at the still water nearby.

"That's right," Mr. Baker nodded. "It's a very large lake, though. It's commonly called a sea, but is bound by land on all sides."

"Well, if lake is the clue, I'm not going back there," Martin said decidedly.

The Bakers and Alec waited in silence for Rich's answer.

"None of us are," he finally decided. "That can't be the proper clue. The clue must be mountain, and we'd better find it or I'll know you've been tricking us."

Rich led a zigzag path, winding through the forest and back to the lake repeatedly because he didn't know what direction to take.

Finally, just when he was getting so frustrated that he was about to accuse the Bakers of misleading him, he came to a place where the trees thinned out and gave way to a grassy plain. There, right before them, were three lush and green hills.

Everybody gave a sigh of relief.

"They're not mountains," Rich grumbled, "but I guess they're the closest things we'll get on this island. Come on."

He led the way again, seemingly not suffering from any fatigue. *He'll stop at nothing until he's found the treasure*, Abby concluded with a sinking heart as she forced her aching legs to stumble forward.

They trudged up the nearest hill, and from there they had a good view of the island and of the sea nearby.

"Next riddle," Rich announced, panting only a little as he turned the page in the leather-bound book. "The place where David hid, with a band of men, from King Saul."

The Bakers exchanged glances. They all knew the answer. Mr. Baker opened his mouth to speak, but Rich quickly said, "And this time, I'm going to choose a person to answer for me. I choose you," he said, pointing to Phil. "You tell me where David hid, with a band of men, from King Saul."

"Uh," Phil began. "David, well, when he was on the run from King Saul...." he trailed off.

"Yes?" Rich prodded. "Hurry up, or I'll know you're bluffing."

Phil swallowed hard. "Er...I...."

"Hurry up!" Rich commanded. "Answer!"

"E-Elah Valley," Phil stammered quickly.

"What?"

"Elah Valley," Phil repeated. "When Saul was king of Israel, David was a young man. His father gave him provisions, which he took to the group of men encamped at Elah Valley. That's where he killed Goliath."

"Ah," Martin nodded in faint recognition.

Rich was frowning, but shrugged. "Well, the clue makes sense, I guess," he said, looking down the side of the hill. "These three hills form a valley in the middle, so let's head down there."

With inward sighs of relief, they all headed down the hill into the valley, which was covered with grass and scattered with little flowers. Andy shot Phil a quick grin to acknowledge the way he had dodged the question and redirected the search.

They got to the bottom of the hill, where Rich instructed them to sit down. "Now listen carefully," he said, looking straight at Abby. "You're going to answer this one. Jesus changed the name of His disciple from Simon, meaning reed, to Peter, meaning ...?"

Abby's mind raced almost as fast as her heart. She glanced quickly at the surrounding hills and then at her father, but Rich immediately scolded her for it.

"Answer the question!" he commanded.

The problem was not that she didn't know the answer, but that she didn't want to give it away. A few seconds passed, and the pressure mounted until she could hardly think at all. Finally, unable to come up with an alternate answer, she hoarsely said, "Stone or rock."

"Yes, that's right," Martin nodded in agreement. "I knew that one, so it was a good test to see if you'd answer correctly or not."

"Stone," Rich repeated. "All right then. You people stay put, and Martin, you watch them. Billy, help me look for a stone or rock."

The two men split up and began searching the hillsides. Abby breathed again as Mr. Baker patted her back comfortingly.

"It'll be all right, Abs," Phil whispered softly.

The sun was starting to go down, and the prisoners watched it sink below the tops of the hills from their position in the valley. The sky turned from orange to pink to purple, and it was starting to get dark when Rich and Billy returned.

"I don't believe there's a single stone on these hillsides that we've left unturned," Rich growled in frustration.

"Don't worry, Rich," Martin said pleasantly. "We can just skip on to the next clue."

"That's the problem," Billy said suddenly, giving the others a bit of a fright. He talked so seldom that when he did, everybody paid attention. "That was the last clue."

Abby drew her breath in surprise, but nobody noticed.

Rich put his hands on his hips and eyed the Bakers angrily. "You must have misled us somewhere," he growled. "Where was it? Where did you try to pull the wool over our eyes, eh?" When he received no answer, he turned on Abby. "Are you sure Peter means stone, little miss? Or did you pull a fast one on us?"

"I tried, but I couldn't think of anything to say," Abby burst out frankly. "Peter means 'stone' or 'rock.' Surely you know that."

"I do," Martin nodded.

"Then why haven't we found the treasure yet?" Rich roared. "Why not?"

"Listen Rich," Mr. Baker said sternly. "I've had enough of you bullying my family. The treasure was buried hundreds of years ago, and has probably been found already. Don't you see how easy it would be to land here, follow the clues, get the treasure, and then place the diary back in the shelter so nobody knows that the treasure is gone?"

"That's exactly what *we* came to do!" Rich shouted.

"Well maybe someone got here first," Phil replied.

"Aargh!" Rich growled, stomping off a few paces. He came back just a minute later. "You're right," he said, to everybody's surprise. The Bakers could see that the cogs in his mind were beginning to turn. "You're right," he said louder. "*You* were here first."

"That's not what I meant," Phil said quickly, realizing what Rich was hinting at.

"What are you saying, Rich?" Martin asked.

"You were here first!" Rich repeated, partly ignoring Martin. "I see it now. You arrived before us and found the treasure, and now you've just been playing tricks on us. Well I've had enough. Tell me where you've put the treasure, before things start getting ugly."

"Yes," Billy agreed coldly.

"We don't have the treasure," Mr. Baker replied.

"We don't even know where it is!" Phil added.

Rich cocked his pistol. "I warned you," he muttered grimly. "Now, you...."

"Wait!" Martin called, jumping to his feet.

Rich and Billy looked up in surprise at Martin's interruption.

"Listen!" he said. "It's the sound of an engine!"

They all held their breaths and clearly heard the sound of a whirring motorboat engine breaking the evening stillness.

Abby looked at her father with wide eyes. "Do you think it's Mother?" she breathed.

Alec overheard and shook his head. "I've got the key to the ignition."

"That had better not be the police," Rich muttered through clenched teeth as he ran up a hill and tried to sight the motorboat. A minute later, he ran down again. "Stand up, all of you. Follow me, and hurry up!"

He started jogging back the way they had come, leading in the direction of the beach. The others followed as quickly as they could, hoping beyond hope that the police had somehow been notified of their plight and had come to rescue them.

They retraced their steps past the lake, along the riverbank, and back towards the beach.

"Lie down!" Rich commanded when they neared the edge of the cliff beside the beach. They all lay on their bellies and peered over the edge. The three thugs had their guns loaded and cocked in readiness.

Down on the beach, a motorboat had been pulled up beside the others and one man was walking up the sand toward the cliff. The Bakers' hearts sank when they saw that the police hadn't come to their rescue after all, but they didn't have much time to consider their disappointment.

"Who are you?" Rich hollered down.

The man paused in his stride, pulled his sunglasses onto the top of his head, and scanned the cliff area where the challenge had come from. Then he replied, in a distinguished British accent, "Richard, Mr. Toole sent me to check your progress. He said you need my help."

The thugs exchanged glances. "No, we don't need any help," Rich replied. "You can tell Mr. Toole we'll have the treasure by tomorrow."

The man on the beach seemed to be chuckling to himself. "I'm afraid you'll have to tell him that yourself when you see him. Tomorrow, as you put it," he added with a laugh. "I can't phone him as there isn't a signal out here; haven't you noticed?"

"I meant you can tell him that when you go back. Right now," Rich replied coldly.

"You can't just send me away, Rich," the man replied. "You're not my employer. I have as much right to be here as you do. Besides, it's too late to go out on the ocean now."

Rich paused. He desperately wanted to get rid of the man, but couldn't think of a way how.

"Come on, Rich," the man continued, resuming his walk up the beach. "You've had plenty of time for this job, and Mr. Toole is getting impatient. Don't be so proud that you refuse my help and regret it afterwards."

"We do need help," Martin blurted quickly.

"Quiet!" Rich hissed angrily. "All right," he finally said. "You have permission to come up."

His permission was a little late in coming, however, as the man was already nearing the cliff.

Rich, Billy, and Martin stood up and commanded the Bakers and Alec to do the same. The men kept their guns in view and appeared to be a little unnerved by their rival.

The stranger found his way up the cliff and paused for a breath at the top, putting his hands on his hips. He was a broad-shouldered, lean man of average height with a hooked nose and shrewd eyes. Altogether, he exuded a presence of affluence and buoyant confidence.

"Hello, gentlemen," he greeted the three thugs pleasantly. "I'm Lewis Nickel, professional treasure-hunter." He extended a hand, which they grudgingly shook. Then, glancing at the Bakers and Alec, he asked, "What have we here?"

"These are our prisoners. They're also after the treasure," Rich answered sulkily.

"Your competition, in other words," Lewis joked with a laugh. The thugs did not appreciate the tinge of truth in his remark, and kept a surly silence. Lewis soon stopped chuckling and put his hands back on his hips. "So, what have you discovered so far?"

"We found a series of riddled clues leading to the treasure," Rich answered hesitantly.

"Ah! This will be easier than I thought," Lewis smiled. "What clue are you on?"

"The last one," Rich answered curtly.

Lewis folded his arms and raised his eyebrows. "Really? So where is this treasure, then?"

The three thugs glanced at each other, and gave Martin a look warning him to keep quiet. "They've got it," Rich replied, pointing to the Bakers and Alec.

"They do?" Lewis asked, looking them up and down. "Where?"

"That's just what we were about to find out when you showed up," Billy's deep voice rumbled.

"Do you mean to suggest that this family found the treasure before you?" Lewis asked incredulously. "They look like tourists!"

"We didn't find it," Mr. Baker quickly said, joining the conversation. "We arrived at the island this morning and discovered Lloyd's shelter and diary. We had been reading the narrative when we heard these men's motorboat engine."

"American," Lewis said to himself, noting Mr. Baker's accent. Martin nodded.

"We hadn't even got to the riddles yet," Mr. Baker finished.

"That must be a lie," Rich growled at Mr. Baker. "If you hadn't read the riddles before, then how could you lead us off track like you did? If you didn't know the island, how could you have led us on a fake trail?"

Lewis frowned. "Led us? I'm sorry, but I think I missed something."

"The clues are riddled so that bad guys don't find the treasure," Martin explained. "We couldn't figure them out by ourselves, so we got these people to help us."

"And we ended up searching a hillside for rocks," Billy rumbled.

"I see," Lewis nodded tactfully. "Well, finding treasure is my specialty. Maybe I can help you with the riddles. May I see them?"

Rich nodded, handing over the leather-bound book hesitantly. "The beginning is just boring diary entries. The clues start about mid-way through."

Lewis paged through the book, studied the first clue, and then looked up. "By the way, have you set up camp yet?"

The thugs looked blankly at one another.

"You do realize that we're going to have to stay overnight, don't you?" he asked by way of explanation.

They nodded slowly, not wanting to give away their lack of forethought.

"We can't make these people traipse around after us in the dark—one or two of them will certainly get away. It would be much more prudent to tie them up somewhere and set a guard over them. That will free us to look for the treasure without distraction," he finished.

"I suppose you're right," Rich agreed.

"You there," Lewis said, calling to Martin, "you look like the guarding type. Tie up these people and make sure you keep a close watch over them. Billy, you help him stay awake. Rich and I will search for the treasure."

"Hey!" Rich bellowed. "I'm in charge of this group, so I give the orders around here! Martin and Billy, you tie up those people and keep a good eye on them. Lewis, you're coming with me to look for the treasure."

Lewis looked put out and surprised at Rich's childish outburst, but he was above arguing. He simply folded his arms and followed as Rich trudged away.

CHAPTER 16

B illy rounded up the Bakers, Alec, and Mrs. Baker and Tom, who had been standing a little way off, while Martin jogged heavily down the slope toward their boat. He returned at a walk, panting heavily, with coils of rope over his shoulder.

While the others had been searching for treasure, Mrs. Baker and Tom had packed away the food and picnic blanket, and they had the two backpacks with them. Billy and Martin allowed them to eat the rest of their food, which wasn't much, before roughly tying their hands and feet and getting them to sit in a circle with their backs in the centre.

Darkness closed in overhead, punctured by a million stars. The Bakers and Alec sat, leaning their backs against each other, for what must have been hours. Billy and Martin took turns to pace and to rest, and their shifts seemed to be the only way to measure the passing of time. Abby closed her eyes and tried to doze, but her hands tied behind her back made sitting awkward and uncomfortable. Her throat was dry, and the aching emptiness of her stomach reminded her that she'd only eaten some crisps and a few carrot sticks for supper.

Whenever she was just drifting off to sleep, she would be awakened by Billy or Martin's torchlight illuminating the darkness and scanning the group.

Then she would look up at the stars, the innumerable beacons of the night sky, and pray for protection from the awesome God Who had created them.

It must have been in the very early hours of the morning that the sound of footsteps awakened Abby from her fitful doze. She opened her eyes to see Martin's torchlight shining on Lewis Nickel's hooked nose as he came up.

"Rich decided to take a rest," he said grumpily as he came closer. "But he told me to bring you two some water."

"Water! Thanks," Martin said as he eagerly took the flask Lewis held out to him. He took a few gulps as Lewis flung himself down on the ground and closed his eyes.

"Tricky riddles, eh?" Martin said sympathetically. Then he handed the flask to Billy, who had woken up at Lewis's approach.

"The riddles aren't the problem," Lewis sighed. "Somebody else is."

"I know what you mean," Martin chuckled, sitting down.

Abby watched as Billy tilted back his head and drank deeply from the flask. Her throat was as dry as sandpaper.

"Could I have a drink, please?" she asked as loudly as she dared.

"What?" Lewis demanded, raising his head from the ground.

"Please could I have a drink?" she repeated nervously.

"Of course not," Lewis answered with such firmness that even Martin seemed surprised. "Refreshment is for those who work, not those who rest. You can wait until morning."

Lewis laid his head back on the ground and resumed his conversation with Martin. "Anyway, as I was saying, *somebody* seems to think *he's* the professional treasure-hunter in this arrangement."

Martin chuckled, leaning his back against a tree. "Oh yes, I can imagine that. He can be a real bossy-boots sometimes," he said, stifling a yawn. "I guess you must be tired."

"Me?" Lewis asked. "Not really. I've had to think so hard for the last few hours that my mind can't stop now." He sat up. "But you look exhausted. Why don't you let me take the rest of your shift?"

Martin thought for a moment. "I am . . . tired," he said, stifling another yawn, "but it's almost Billy's turn now." He turned and poked the man, and then shook him hard, with no effect. "Oh, he's sound asleep. If you take his shift, he'll be very grateful. As for me, I really do need a rest."

"All right then," Lewis said, standing up. "Shall I wake you up when it's your turn again?"

"Yeah," Martin nodded sleepily as he handed Lewis his torch and then stretched himself out on the grass. "Thanks, Lewis," he finished, his voice trailing off drowsily.

A minute later, steady breathing came from both of the men. Lewis prodded Martin gently, and when there was no response, he pulled something from his own pocket and strode toward the huddled prisoners.

Phil, who was beside Abby, stiffened as the man approached, especially when he saw the glint of steel in his hand.

Lewis knelt down when he reached Phil, who was closest. He set down the torch and began severing the bonds around Phil's ankles with the Swiss army knife in his hand. At first Phil seemed too surprised to say anything, but soon he whispered, "What . . . what are you doing?"

"I'm freeing you," Lewis stated matter-of-factly. "You need to find the treasure as soon as you can. Please turn around, Phil, so I can free your hands."

Phil immediately did as he was told, but his jaw was slack. "How do you know my name?" he whispered.

"You don't have to whisper," Lewis replied. "Those two will sleep soundly for a few solid hours. And speaking of that," he paused as he finished cutting through Phil's bonds, "here's a little water for Abby to drink." With that, he handed his knife to Phil and pulled from his top pocket a small flask.

"You doped Martin and Billy?" Phil asked incredulously as he took the flask from Lewis.

"Yes, of course," Lewis replied. "That's why I couldn't let any of you drink that water. I'm sorry, Abby, for my nasty response earlier, but it was necessary."

"That's okay," was all Abby managed to reply as Phil cut through the ropes around her wrists.

Lewis, in the meantime, had pulled out a smaller knife and started freeing Mr. Baker with it. "I brought provisions in my boat," he said. "All of you must be hungry."

"Detective Mortimer?" Mr. Baker asked uncertainly.

"No," Lewis shook his head. "The detective had to stay in Hertfordshire to clear matters up. That's why he sent me to rescue you."

Abby looked at the man with a frown. "Mr. Jigson?"

"I was just about to make the same suggestion," Phil agreed.

Lewis laughed. "I'm surprised anyone could recognize me with this horrendous false nose on."

"We didn't recognize you," Phil chuckled. "It's just that we couldn't think of anyone else who knows our names."

"Out of all the undercover agents we know, we narrowed it down to you," Andy added dryly with a grin as Lewis, or rather Jigson, freed his hands.

"Where's Rich?" Mr. Baker asked.

"Asleep by the lake. He's also been sedated," Jigson replied. "There are a few hours before daybreak. Let's hope we've found the treasure by then."

Jigson and Phil finished freeing everybody, and Alec and Jigson were introduced. Then, at Jigson's suggestion, Billy and Martin were bound hand and foot with the rope that had been used on the Bakers.

"Let's bring a coil or two for Rich," he added.

They set out, with Jigson leading the way towards the lake. When they got to the brook, he suggested that Mr. Baker take the group straight to the three hills rather than leading everybody along the slippery bank. Some members of the group were particularly relieved that they wouldn't have to scramble along the sloping, muddy path in the dark.

Phil decided to accompany Jigson to the lake, so the two of them set off while Mr. Baker led the way around the forest, keeping parallel to the river. Sure enough, the Bakers came to the three hills and sat down to wait there for Phil and Jigson. The sky was already growing faintly light by the time the two of them appeared.

"We found Rich just as I left him," Jigson said, "and bound him tightly. We also found Lloyd's diary in his pocket."

"Great," Mr. Baker said as Jigson handed the diary to him. "We can look through the riddles and give the real answers."

Jigson nodded. "I've been looking at those riddles all night, so I know them all well. The first one was about the brook Cherith. The second referred to the lake of fire. Next came the one about lifting our eyes to the hills." He paused and looked at Andy with a laugh. "Rich told me that you said the answer was trees."

Andy chuckled as he nodded.

"If we go in sequence," Jigson said, resuming his serious tone, "we should follow the brook till we get to the lake, and then move on to the hills, which is where we are now."

"The next clue was about Jesus calming the storm on the Sea of Galilee," Mr. Baker continued. "I assume that means we should head toward the sea."

"Yes," Jigson agreed.

They walked toward the sea, where they found the island drop steeply in a cliff to the rocks below.

"The next clue is about David hiding from Saul," Phil said. "I remember because I had to answer that one. I said Elah Valley, but really David hid in a cave."

"A cave!" Abby said with a look of realization. "There must be one somewhere in this cliff."

"But the tide is coming in," Mrs. Baker pointed out. "There's no way we could go down there safely now."

She was right. Waves splashed forcefully over the rocks and foamed up against the cliff face.

"We'll just have to wait for the tide to go out," Phil suggested.

"I'm afraid we can't," Jigson said in a low voice. He paused as he looked at the puzzled faces around him. "I posed as Lewis Nickel, a professional treasure hunter sent by Mr. Toole to help find the Jenkins treasure," he paused again. "The real Lewis Nickel could arrive at any moment. And unlike me, he's coming with two accomplices."

Shaken expressions replaced the puzzled ones as the Bakers realized the danger of their predicament.

"That's why we have to find the treasure and leave this island as soon as possible," Jigson finished.

"So what do you suggest?" Mr. Baker asked, recovering from his surprise.

"We should take the motorboats to this side of the island and search the cliff face for a cave. I believe the last clue is stone, so there must be a particular stone or rock inside the cave that leads to the treasure. I'll look for it when I swim inside the cave."

"That sounds dangerous!" Mrs. Baker said. "You could be dashed on the rocks, or trapped inside the cave by the incoming tide."

"It's possible," Jigson nodded, "but that's the only plan I can think of. Taking risks is, after all, part of my job."

"Well, then," Mr. Baker said, "we had better get started."

Jigson nodded. "I discovered a shortcut to the motorboats. Please follow me."

They followed him in a direct route to the cliff sloping down to the beach, and didn't stop until they came to the boats.

"That small boat there is mine," Jigson pointed, "so one of these two must be yours," he said, turning to Alec.

"Yes, this one is mine," he said, patting the nearest boat.

"Can you disable the other one?" Mr. Baker asked.

Alec nodded confidently and set to work right away.

While Alec was busy with the thugs' boat, Jigson darted inside his cabin to get the provisions he had mentioned earlier. "There isn't enough room in here for so many people, I'm afraid, so some of us will have to eat outside."

If any of them minded eating breakfast on the sandy beach in the chilly air, they were too hungry to show it.

"I don't have much," Jigson continued, handing out sealed packets of crackers and some cereal bars, "but at least we can eat this on the go. I also brought bottles of fresh water."

After quickly eating the crackers and drinking some water, the Bakers, Jigson, and Alec pushed the boats across the sand to where the waves lapped around their knees. Alec and the Bakers boarded Alec's boat, while Phil and Jigson boarded the other one.

The whirring of engines added to the rushing sound of the waves on the sand as Jigson and Alec started the two boats and began steering them out of the bay. They traveled around the rocks toward the side of the island the clues had directed them to. They slowed down when they neared the cliff face and began searching it for signs of a cave. The rocks forming the cliff face were dark and jagged, and there appeared to be indents in the rocks everywhere, which were easy to mistake as caves.

Finally, Jigson and Phil heard a holler from the other boat, which was a good distance away. They looked over to see the Mr. Baker and Andy waving their arms and pointing toward the cliff. Mr. Baker had his hands cupped around his mouth and called something, but the wind whipped the message into a jumble.

"They must have found the cave," Phil said as Jigson started the boat engine and began speeding along the water. The sun had already risen and was shining brightly.

When Jigson's boat neared the other one, Mr. Baker called, "We found the cave!" Andy pointed enthusiastically to an area in the cliff face on the other side of their boat, and Jigson steered his boat to that spot.

"Our boat looks small enough to fit in there," Jigson called after studying the cave for a few seconds.

"I don't think this boat will make it," Mr. Baker said.

Jigson shook his head. "Alec's is too wide. Well, I'm going in—Phil, are you coming along?"

"Yes, I'd like to," Phil nodded eagerly.

"Well, I'd be grateful for your help." Then, turning to the other boat, Jigson said, "Perhaps you can warn us of anybody coming or of a dangerously high tide."

Mr. Baker nodded in agreement, and then Andy quickly called, "Have you got a torch?"

"Yes," Jigson replied with a nod. "It's Martin's one." With that, he began moving the boat gently forward, being careful not to have it strike the rocks on the cliff face. He eased the boat into the rather narrow crack in the cliff, and Phil switched the torch on to compensate for the fast-dwindling light.

Jigson navigated the narrow passage of water carefully, dodging the rocks on either side, while Phil shone the torch to help. The water became gradually shallower as they ventured further into the cave, until the boat ran aground on a sandy beach with an extremely high roof. Phil and Jigson leapt out the boat and pulled it as far as they could, finally fastening it by rope to a sturdy rock.

"The tide will continue coming in," Jigson explained, "and the last thing we want is for our boat to come loose and float away."

Phil handed the torch to Jigson. They walked along the sand, keeping their eyes peeled for any sign of a notable rock or stone which Lloyd could have referred to in his clue. The cave became gradually narrower and narrower, and the roof lower and lower, until Phil and Jigson had to walk in single file through a tight corridor of rock that wound uphill steeply.

"Do you think we've gone too far, and traveled right past Lloyd's rock?" Phil asked.

"I have no idea," Jigson answered. "All we can do is continue looking and pray that we find it soon."

After a while, the narrow corridor leveled out and opened onto a wide chamber with a high, domed roof. Both Phil and Jigson gave sighs of relief to be out of that miserable, uphill squeeze, and quickly admired the place they found themselves in. Jigson swung the torch around, studying the rock formations that the dancing torchlight exposed.

"If only Andy was here with his camera," Phil whispered, his voice echoing off the walls.

They wandered around the chamber for what felt like a very long time, examining crevices in the walls and floor. They had almost completed their circuit of the room when there was a panting sound from the direction of the entrance, which echoed around the chamber.

Jigson and Phil were immediately on their guard, and Jigson flicked off the torch. He waited a few seconds, and then switched the torch on again, beaming it directly at the entrance and dazzling a wet face.

"Andy!" Phil exclaimed as he recognized his brother. "What are you doing here?"

Jigson quickly diverted the torchlight so that it wasn't in the boy's eyes as he crawled up the last stretch and into the cavern, his chest heaving. Phil was by his side in an instant, helping him into a sitting position with his back against the wall. His hair was plastered to his head.

"What happened?" Phil asked. "Why are you so wet?"

"The real Lewis Nickel arrived," Andy gasped. "I think he's captured the others. I've come to warn you."

Jigson and Phil's faces grew serious as they heard the news.

"The tide has come in a lot, and some of the tunnel is flooded. I had to swim up a long section of that narrow corridor. I was afraid I wouldn't make it."

"Goodness!" Phil exclaimed. "That was brave."

"Yes, well done!" Jigson agreed. Then, he asked, "How did the others get captured?"

"We heard the whirring of a boat engine," Andy said, becoming able to speak without panting, "so we called and called you from the mouth of the cave, but got no response. That's when I volunteered to find you. Father, and especially Mother, was hesitant to let me go because of the rise in the tide, but there didn't seem to be any other way to tell you. Father wanted to stay with the others in case Lewis found them. Our parents have no idea how flooded the tunnel is," Andy said. "By the time I had swum a little way into the cave with a high roof, I heard the sound of loud voices in conversation. I stayed there, behind a rock, and heard most of the exchange. It ended when both boats sped away in the direction of the beach. I knew then that I was the only one who could get the message to you, so I knew I had to take the risks involved."

CHAPTER 17

"Well, we're in quite a predicament," Phil commented as Andy finished.

Jigson nodded soberly. "If they find me, they'll know I'm an undercover agent. And they'll show no mercy. Believe me, Lewis Nickel has a nasty reputation."

"So what are we going to do?" Phil asked.

"Well," Jigson paused, "it's only a matter of time before we are found."

"What do you mean?" Andy asked.

"Your father has Lloyd's diary, and I'm sure once Rich wakes up, he'll realize it's not in his pocket anymore. He'll probably find it, and once he hands that diary to Lewis, it won't be long before all of them are outside the cave entrance, blocking our escape."

"Then we should find the treasure and go, before they can block us," Phil said urgently.

"We can't leave now," Andy answered with a shake of his head. "The water level will have risen even more. We'd never be able to hold our breaths all the way to the entrance, especially not if we have to take the treasure with us. We have to wait for the tide to go out."

"And by then, it'll be too late to escape," Jigson added.

"So we're trapped in here," Phil concluded.

Jigson nodded slowly. "We're trapped inside by the tide, and our enemies are trapped outside by the tide." His voice trailed off as he thought.

"Mr. Jigson?" Andy finally asked.

"Hmm?"

"If the bad guys do find the treasure, what will they do to us?"

Jigson paused. "The kindest thing they would do is maroon your family here."

"That's the *kindest* thing?" Andy asked. "And what would happen to you?"

Jigson shook his head slowly. "I'm working undercover, Andy. That means taking the greatest risks and being in the greatest danger." He paused. "Come on. We don't have any time to lose. We have to find the treasure and figure out a way to escape before the tide goes out. I don't like to think what will happen otherwise."

The three of them stood up with renewed energy and a sense of urgency, and they determined to search the cavern again for any sign of a prominent stone or rock. From Jigson's calculations, there were only a few hours before the tide went out low enough for the thugs to enter the cave.

They had searched tirelessly for some time when Phil suddenly pointed up the wall to a large, grey rock which contrasted with the surrounding masses of black rock. He reached up and tugged at the grey rock, which was wedged neatly in a crevice in the rock face. Jigson handed Andy the torch, and then helped Phil pull hard at the rock.

With a loud 'crack' that reverberated around the cavern, the rock suddenly came loose from what was presumably hundreds of years of residence in the rock face, revealing a large niche in the wall. Phil clambered up the wall a short distance to get a better view inside the niche, and asked Jigson for the torch. He pulled the torch up to the rim of the niche and gasped in excitement as he caught sight of a dark-colored, square object that had an ancient bit of frayed rope tied around its middle.

"What is it?" Andy asked in breathless excitement.

"It's Lloyd's chest all right," Phil replied. "His rope is still attached! Now the problem is getting it down safely."

He handed the torch to Jigson and then used both hands to pull at the chest, his feet balancing on a rocky section of the wall.

He pulled and strained, and finally shook his head. "No, it's too heavy for me to move from this angle."

He stepped down, allowing Andy and Jigson to see it.

"That must be the rope Lloyd used," Andy said. "I'm amazed it still exists."

"Look how old and worn this chest is," Jigson added. "I wonder how strong it is after all these years. Do you know where the key is?"

"Lloyd didn't have a key," Phil answered, "but somehow he opened it without one."

"Hmm," Jigson muttered in thought. "Well there's no point in spending time opening it now. The thugs musn't get their hands on it, and that means we have to find a way of escape."

"It'll be quite some time before the tide is low enough for us to swim back to the boat," Phil wondered aloud.

"Especially weighted down with the chest," Jigson said. "If I'm correct, the cave entrance is at water level at high tide. The tunnel that leads here slopes steeply upward, so we're probably not very far below the surface."

"People could be walking above us right now, and we wouldn't know it," Andy said, "and we could be below them right now, and they don't know it."

"I've just thought of something!" Phil suddenly exclaimed. "Can you hand me the torch?"

He switched it on and shone the light at the niche the chest was in, again clambering a little way up the rocky wall for a better look. "Yes, I'm right! I didn't notice properly before, but there's a small opening at the back of this niche," he said. "Maybe it leads out of here."

"Would you like me to explore it?" Andy volunteered. "I'm smaller than you, so I'm less likely to get stuck if the tunnel narrows or ends."

"All right," Phil agreed, jumping down. "But be careful, Andy. Don't continue if the way looks dangerous."

He gave Andy a leg up, and the boy climbed into the niche and over the chest. Since his torch didn't work after being submerged in water, Jigson handed him Martin's, reminding him that it was precious as their only light source.

Then Andy started crawling through the tunnel in the side of the niche wall. For a while, Phil and Jigson could see the glow of light from the little tunnel, but when Andy rounded a corner the cavern became dark again.

"Even if that tunnel doesn't lead anywhere," Jigson mused, "at least we have a hiding place in that niche. It might buy us a little time, but unfortunately that's all it'll do. Lewis Nickel will find us eventually. Besides, we'd have to get food and water before long."

"Does Lewis Nickel really look like your disguise?" Phil asked.

"Yes," Jigson answered with a short laugh. "Just meaner."

They stood there in the darkness for what felt like an hour. Their only pastimes were whistling down the tunnel to Andy and hearing him whistle back, and groping in the darkness to the cavern entrance to try judge the water level. The darkness became tangible, and felt like it was closing in and wrapping itself around them like a big, dark blanket. The cheery whistles from Andy that echoed down the tunnel seemed out-of-place in the overwhelming darkness.

Finally, it was Jigson's turn to whistle down the tunnel, and there was no reply. He and Phil waited and waited, sending whistles down at regular intervals, but all they heard was their own echoes.

"I wonder if he's stuck," Phil said worriedly.

"He would still whistle back," Jigson replied, his normally-confident voice strained too. "Maybe he's gone so far that he can't hear us anymore."

"Then he would be wondering why we've stopped whistling. Do you think I should go down and make sure he's all right?"

Jigson paused. "Let's wait a little longer before taking action."

They waited some minutes more, whistling regularly down the tunnel, when they finally heard a faint one in response. It sounded less cheery and more urgently determined than before. The whistles from the tunnel grew gradually louder, though shorter and more direct as though Andy was out of breath.

Finally, Phil and Jigson could hear panting as Andy crawled nearer, and then the light of the torch glowing as he rounded the last bend.

"I'm so glad you're back!" Phil said. Not only had his brother returned, but also the torchlight, which vastly improved the appearance of the situation.

"The tunnel leads all the way out of here," Andy said between gasps for breath. "It gets quite narrow at places, but I think you'll both fit."

"That's good news," Jigson said, "but we're going to have to take the chest with us and somehow leave a fake clue to keep our friend Lewis busy. Any ideas?"

"If we had paint we could put a great, big 'x' on the wall," Andy said.

"Or we could just wedge this grey rock, the real clue, into the wall somewhere else," Phil suggested.

"Let's do that," Jigson answered.

"How will we block up the hole after us?" Andy asked.

"It'll probably be less noticeable if we don't block it up," Jigson said. "There are other recesses in the wall of this cavern, and hopefully nobody will assume that this one was *the one* Lloyd used to hide the treasure."

As quickly as they could, Phil and Jigson searched for a spot near the ground to plant the grey rock as a false lead. With that done, Phil and Jigson climbed up the rock face into the niche. Phil was wearing a belt, so he took it off and fastened it to the chest. That way, he could pull it from the front and Jigson could push it from behind. With their combined effort, they found that they could edge the chest along.

"I'm astounded at the weight of such a small chest," Phil said. "It's no bigger than a large shoebox, and yet feels like it weighs a ton!"

Jigson nodded. "It feels like gold to me."

They traveled along the tunnel in that fashion, scraping their hands and knees on the rough stone below, and sometimes knocking their heads on the low roof above. The tunnel seemed to go on and on, but fortunately Andy was able to encourage them along and warn them of features in the tunnel ahead.

"Andy," Phil said, panting, "at one stage we were whistling to you and there was no response. Were you too far away to hear us?"

"No," Andy answered, shining the torch backwards as Phil and Jigson pulled and shoved the chest over a rocky bit. "I didn't reply because I had come to the end of the tunnel and was looking out on a grassy hillside with the sea to my left. I was worried that if anybody was around, they might hear me."

"Good thinking," Jigson approved as they battled onward. Andy turned the torch ahead so he could see where he was going. Fortunately, the light did bounce off the walls and somewhat lit up the way for Phil and Jigson to follow.

They continued on and on along the tunnel, going upwards and downwards, and turning left and right around bends. Phil and Jigson tried their utmost not to damage the chest, which made the task much more laborious.

Finally, when Jigson was just about to ask for the torch to check his watch, the tunnel became brighter, and, coming around a corner, they saw light coming from between long blades of grass at a round hole.

"We're nearly there," Andy whispered.

Phil and Jigson began moving the chest very slowly and quietly until Jigson whispered, "Let's leave it here until we've had a chance to see where we are."

Phil nodded his agreement, and they turned the chest sideways so that Jigson could crawl past it. Then they moved forward to join Andy as he cautiously peered through the long grass at the entrance.

"I can't see anyone," he breathed. "Hopefully the coast is clear."

"I think I had better go first," Jigson whispered.

The other two nodded and made room for Jigson to pass. He looked carefully through the grass, and then pulled it gently aside. After a short while, he started crawling through the opening until he was completely out, and he motioned for the two brothers to follow him.

Phil and Andy left the tunnel quickly and quietly, and found themselves on a grassy hillside with the sea pounding the cliff to their left, just as Andy had described. The sun was warm and already high in the sky, and was a heavenly, though stark, change from the dark cave.

They looked around to try and spot Jigson, who had apparently disappeared. Then Phil tapped Andy's arm and pointed to some trees a short distance away. Andy followed Phil's finger to see Jigson leaning out from behind a tree, motioning for them to follow. They hurried to the clump of trees, and both chose ones to hide behind.

"Good," Jigson breathed as he reached up and started climbing his tree, making use of branches and mounting higher and higher at a surprising pace. Phil and Andy quickly caught on to the idea and began climbing their own trees. Andy, however, was smaller, more nimble, and better practiced than Phil and Jigson, and he shot up his tree like a monkey.

From the top of his tree, Jigson surveyed the area to see where they were, and if there were people around. They were beside a grassy hill, and no people were visible.

He glanced at his watch. "8:45," he muttered to himself. "The sedative will have worn off by now." Then, a little louder, he said, "You two, please keep a look-out. Give some kind of bird call if you see somebody."

Phil and Andy turned and nodded, and scanned the area from their perches at the tops of the trees. Jigson, in the meantime, climbed down his tree and began sprinting to the cliff edge as fast as he could. Phil and Andy saw him kneel and peer downwards for some time before jogging back to the trees. Phil came down to hear the report.

"The tide is well out," Jigson said. "I can see footprints in the sand down there, heading toward the cave entrance. I'd say they were made by about five people – either by your family and Alec, or, more likely, they were made by Lewis Nickel and some accomplices. In the latter case, your family members are probably being kept somewhere, and we have to find them."

Phil nodded in understanding. "Should Andy stay here as look-out?"

Jigson thought for a moment. "Yes, I think that will be best." He lowered his voice. "It'll also keep him out of danger."

Phil gave a discreet nod, and then motioned for Andy to come down the tree.

"Andy," Jigson said in a serious tone, "we need you to stay here as look-out for us, so you can warn us if you see anything dangerous. Can you make an unobtrusive bird call?"

"I can do an owl hoot," Andy answered.

Jigson frowned. "Owls don't hoot in daytime."

"What about your pigeon imitation?" Phil suggested. Andy had a knack for making some of the best pigeon calls in his family.

"All right," he nodded confidently before giving Jigson a demonstration. He clasped his hands tightly together, trapping a pocket of air between them. Then he lined up his thumbs and blew between them.

"Perfect," Jigson said approvingly at the resulting pigeon-like sound. Then he and Phil crept cautiously away and Andy climbed back up his tree.

CHAPTER 18

A bby sat with her knees drawn up and her head resting miserably on them. Once again, she and her family were imprisoned with Martin as their guard. They had each been given some water to drink and a little food from the thugs' provisions, but the empty, gnawing feeling in Abby's stomach could hardly be ignored.

The sun was shining brightly, and normally she would have considered the weather ideal for being outdoors. But being made to sit, unmoving, in the hot sun, was very unpleasant.

After Andy had swum into the cave to warn Phil and Jigson that morning, the real Lewis Nickel and his accomplices had suddenly appeared. Having heard about the Bakers from his boss, Lewis was understandably surprised to see them free, in a boat off the coast of the island, with Rich nowhere in sight. He had challenged them, asking them who they were and why they were there.

Mr. Baker had replied that they were a tourist family from America, but Lewis wasn't satisfied and had commanded them to return to the beach with him. Mr. Baker considered trying to zip away and escape, but Alec assured him that the other boat was faster and would certainly catch up with them before they reached the Cornish coast. The men with Lewis had nasty expressions and looked like they wouldn't hesitate to use force to get what they wanted. Further, Mr. Baker didn't like the idea of leaving Jigson, and especially Phil and Andy, behind. So they compliantly followed Lewis's boat to the shore, tied up the boat again, and returned to the island with great anxiety.

Much sooner than the Bakers would have liked, the whole party stumbled across Billy and Martin, who were still suffering the effects of the sedative, and were barely awake. Lewis immediately suspected the Bakers of doping them, despite Mr. Baker's protests to the contrary. Technically, Jigson had done it, so the Bakers could plead innocence in good conscience.

Lewis, however, set out with two men to find Rich, leaving three others to watch the Bakers and Alec. All the time they spent waiting, the Bakers wondered what had happened to Andy, and where Phil and Jigson were. Had they found the treasure? Had Andy been able to deliver the message?

After a good half hour, Billy and Martin were sufficiently awake to realize what had happened. About this time, Lewis and his men returned with Rich, helping to prop him up as he staggered along. Having been drugged first, Rich was the first one to recover. He told Lewis the story from his perspective, and Lewis was enraged that somebody had pretended to be him. The Bakers and Alec were relieved that Jigson wasn't there at that moment.

Lloyd's diary was discovered on Mr. Baker's person, and Lewis, his five comrades, and Rich all set out to follow the clues, leaving Martin again as guard and posting Billy at the boats as look-out.

Soon afterwards, Martin ate his breakfast and was considerate enough to give his prisoners some of the provisions that were left over.

Almost two hours had passed since then, and Abby groaned inwardly as the harsh sun beat down on them. *How long must we wait, Lord?* she had called out to God. *Please do something miraculous soon! And keep Phil, Andy, and Mr. Jigson safe from these villains.*

A stomping noise filled the air, heralding the arrival of Lewis, Rich, and the five other men.

"Did you find the treasure?" Martin ventured to ask the intimidating man in front of him.

"Almost," Lewis replied with a snarl. "We're going to need a little assistant," he said, casting his eyes over the Bakers.

They looked up in surprise, wondering what he might mean. They didn't have to wonder for long.

"You there," he called, looking at Abby. "Stand up."

Abby's eyes widened as she was singled out, and she rose nervously to her feet.

"You're coming with us," Lewis said. "And you too," he added, nodding at Mr. Baker.

Mr. Baker spoke everyone's mind as he asked, "What for?"

"If you must know," Lewis paused, "we found a little tunnel that must be explored. And none of us think we're small enough to fit inside."

Mr. Baker opened his mouth to speak, but then closed it again. He and Abby were prodded along as they followed Lewis and Rich back the way they had come.

They walked to the beach, passing Billy as they did so, and walked a far distance across the sand before climbing aboard Lewis's motorboat. The tide had gone out so far that the boat had been tied up a good distance from the cliff.

The boat was steered out of the bay and turned to the place where the Bakers had been caught earlier that day. The trip took a few minutes, and Abby was surprised to see that the receding tide had left the cave exposed to view. The waves didn't even touch the cliff.

All of the passengers, except one of Lewis's men, jumped out of the boat into the shallow water near the cliff. The last man steered the boat into a sheltered niche in the rocks and fastened it there before re-joining the group.

They entered the cave on foot, when several of the men switched on flashlights. They had traveled a little over five minutes when the cave roof lowered drastically and Abby and Mr. Baker caught sight of the motorboat Phil and Jigson had used earlier. Abby paled when she realized they might have already been caught by Lewis.

Lewis shone his light on the abandoned motorboat and looked at Mr. Baker with a smirk. "Just tourists, eh?"

Mr. Baker did not reply.

"Lee, you watch that boat, as before," Lewis instructed. One of the men obediently split off from the group and stood guard at the boat while the others carried on walking through the cave.

Soon, the cave narrowed so much that it became necessary to walk in single file. Lewis was leading the group, followed by Rich and two men. Then came Abby and Mr. Baker, followed by two more men.

Abby noticed, as she walked, that the tunnel sloped sharply uphill. The group walked steadily onwards for some time in the narrow tunnel. The broader men tried not to show their difficulty, or claustrophobia, in so doing.

Then, without warning, the tunnel became level and opened out onto a huge cavern. Abby took a deep breath as she gazed at the place, illuminated by torchlight. As soon as all the men had caught their breath, Lewis resumed his treasure-hunting mission.

"Little girl," he announced, his cunning eyes looking down his beak-like nose, "we discovered a small tunnel in one of the walls in this cavern; it's a route that your friends must have used to escape this place. What I want you to do is to crawl down that tunnel until you get to the end of it. Then come back and tell us what you've found. If you find the treasure, bring it back with you, because we're all going to stay in this miserable hole until we find it." He stopped speaking, as though that was all he had to say. Then he lowered his voice to a threatening growl that reverberated around the cavern. "And if you don't come back," he paused, "we'll harm your dad."

Abby's jaw slackened at the threat, and she nodded feebly in understanding. She shot a last look at her father as she was prodded toward the cavern wall. At quite a distance up was a rock ledge and the entrance to a small tunnel. A torch was pushed into her hand, and she trembled like a leaf as she was hoisted up towards the niche. She didn't think she would be able to pull herself into it because she was shaking so much, but somehow she found the strength to do it.

"Now," Lewis instructed, "listen carefully. As you explore the tunnel, call back to us every five minutes to let us know you haven't given us the slip. Because you know what will happen if we think that, don't you?"

Abby nodded and gulped.

"Then off you go," Lewis finished with a shooing motion of his hands.

Abby switched on the torch she had been given and began crawling down the tunnel. Though the entrance was narrow, the tunnel was certainly wide enough for her, and she was sure that a man would be able to travel down it quite easily. However, she was not about to go back and tell Lewis that. She thought about what he had said. *'We discovered a small tunnel. . . . it's a route that your friends must have used to escape this place.' Our friends—those are Phil, Mr. Jigson, and Andy. Could they really have escaped down this very tunnel? What if it's a dead end?* Then another thought struck her. *If it is a dead end, could they still be in here, waiting for a chance to get out?*

She sped up her crawling until she scraped her hand badly on a sharp rock and decided it was time to call back to Lewis and his men.

"I'm still here!" she called, cupping her hands around her mouth. The sound was loud and hollow as it bounced off the walls of the tunnel. She waited for a reply. After a few seconds, she heard Lewis's voice boom, "Go on!"

She resumed her crawling, picking her way carefully in an effort not to hurt her bleeding hand. At some points, the tunnel roof was high enough for her to walk doubled over. She tried this, but had to bend over so far that she soon decided that crawling was more comfortable.

She continued for what seemed like a long time, stopping every few minutes to holler back down the tunnel. *Forward, forward, forward!* she encouraged herself. *"My grace is sufficient for thee: for my strength is made perfect in weakness,"* she recited.

On and on she crawled down the long tunnel, over sharp rocks and loose stones, up inclines and around corners, until she rounded a last bend and found herself gazing at a grass-covered hole, and, more surprisingly, an old, square object.

"The treasure chest," she muttered in awe and surprise as she ran the torchlight over it. "It's right here," she breathed as she pulled herself forward to run her fingers along the old chest. It was roughly two feet long, one foot wide, and one foot high. Remembering the urgency of her mission, she called and whistled loudly down the tunnel and then carried on crawling towards the patch of sunlight at the exit.

She looked through the grass growing across the entrance, and then moved it aside as she pushed her head through the hole. The warm sunlight was blinding, and she had to close her eyes tightly for a few seconds. In that time she heard an alarmed bird-call and her heart skipped a beat. She opened her eyes and squinted at the trees the call had come from. The leaves of one of them was shaking, and suddenly the figure of a boy dropped out of it onto the ground. He peered out from behind the trunk and motioned urgently for Abby to come closer.

With a feeling of ecstasy, Abby crawled out the hole and sprinted to the clump of trees. "Andy!" she exclaimed as she gave her twin brother a hug. "You're safe!"

"Yes, yes, but what about you? How on earth did you happen to come out that hole? And what happened to your hand?"

As quickly as she could, Abby poured out the tale. "So you see, I have to get back as soon as I can. And I have to take the chest with me," she finished. "If I don't, we'll be stuck in the cavern forever."

Andy nodded in thought. "I see."

"But it's so heavy that I'm not sure I can take it all that way quick enough," Abby added.

"I've got an idea!" Andy suddenly cried, grabbing Abby's arm and pulling her back toward the tunnel. "Follow me."

They ran back to the hill and slipped into the hole. There, with pounding hearts, they examined the chest and Andy pulled out the pen-knife Grandfather Wilson had given him.

Abby whistled down the tunnel before asking softly, "What's your idea?"

"This is it," Andy began. "You can't take this chest back on your own, and I can't help you because I'm supposed to be on look-out duty for Phil and Mr. Jigson. Besides, we don't want the bad guys to get the treasure. This is what I suggest. Let's pry the chest open and empty out all the treasure right here. You drag back an empty chest and fill it with loose rocks as you go along. Then, when you get close to the cavern, you close the chest carefully and put on an innocent expression."

"Oh Andy, that sounds very adventurous, but I'm not sure it'll work," Abby replied. "How will we get the chest open in the first place?"

"Lloyd got it open without a key," Andy replied, "so there must be a way."

"Then, as for looking innocent, I'm not sure I can put on a false expression. Besides, what if Lewis decides to open the chest right then and there?"

"You're only a kid, Abby!" Andy countered. "Even if he did open the chest, he'd never suspect that you, a girl, formulated such a brilliant plan. He'd think it was Lloyd Jenkins playing a trick on treasure-hunters."

Though Abby didn't quite agree with Andy's reasoning, she couldn't think of another plan. Andy began examining the chest for a way to open it with his penknife, and Abby again called and whistled loudly down the tunnel, hoping that Lewis was staying true to his agreement.

The chest was an old one, yet the padlock and the latch it attached to were so sturdy that Andy couldn't budge them no matter how hard he tried. "You'll have to pick the lock," Abby said. "It's not about to fall apart."

Andy took his sister's suggestion and slid the point of his knife into the keyhole. He fiddled for a while, twisting and turning the knife, before shaking his head. "That's not going to work." He tilted his head and studied the chest once more before whispering excitedly, "I've got it! I'll take off the hinges! That *must* have been what Lloyd did."

He moved the chest so he had a good view of the hinges, which were held in place by nails. He started sliding his knife under one of the nail-heads, and his muscles tensed as he tried to pry the nail out of its hole.

"Oh," he muttered, "this is very stiff."

"We have to get help," Abby concluded, glancing nervously at her watch and peering out the hole.

"No, we'll be fine," Andy said. "This nail is loosening; I'm sure I can feel it."

"Where's Phil?"

"I don't know," Andy replied. "He and Mr. Jigson went looking for you and the others."

"I know where they're being kept by Martin," Abby said. "I'll sneak back there and hopefully find Phil or Mr. Jigson on the way."

"Oh, all right," Andy agreed. "I'll continue trying while you're away."

Abby whistled again down the tunnel. "If I'm not back in five minutes," she said, "please whistle to Lewis for me."

She slipped cautiously out the tunnel into the warm sunshine again. After momentarily pausing to adjust her eyes and get her bearings, she crept quietly in the direction of Martin and the prisoners.

When she arrived there, Martin was standing up, tense and surprised, with his gun trained on a nearby bush.

"Put your hands in the air and come out slowly," he commanded, "and I won't shoot."

Abby watched as one pair of hands appeared from behind the bush, and Phil stood up slowly and steadily.

"Come out from behind there," Martin called, "and sit down where I can see you."

Abby's heart sank as her brother walked towards his family members and sat down beside them. Martin seemed unnerved by this incident, and he didn't stop looking uneasily over his shoulder.

Abby feared he might spot her, so, as quietly as she could, she picked her way back to the hillside. She was almost there when she heard a realistic birdcall a little way behind her. She stopped suddenly, turning to scan the bushes.

"Mr. Jigson!" she breathed as the fake Lewis Nickel appeared. "Thank the Lord you're safe! Andy and I desperately need some help."

As quickly as she could, Abby re-told her story. As she did so, Jigson's face became grim. She finished with Andy's idea of opening the chest.

"This is serious business," Jigson muttered, deep in thought. "Andy's idea is a good one; however, it's dangerous too."

"Uh, Mr. Jigson?"

"Yes?"

"Phil's capture—that was planned, wasn't it?" Abby asked hesitantly.

"Not exactly," Jigson said and shook his head before turning towards the hole. He and Abby crawled through it to find Andy still trying to remove the nails.

"Let me have a go," Jigson whispered, pulling out his Swiss army knife. Andy folded his slightly bent penknife and put it in his pocket. He moved aside to make room for Jigson and watched as the man placed one hand on the chest and slid the knife under a nail-head with the other. He pulled hard on that knife for a few moments, until there was a sudden 'crack' and the nail-head sheared off.

"Hmm," he muttered before moving onto the next nail. That one seemed looser than the first, and he was able to pull it out with only a little difficulty.

"It's not rusted," he said as he glanced at the nail in the palm of his hand. "I wonder if it's made of brass."

He handed it to Andy and took a breath before moving onto the next nail. Some of them were less stiff than others, and within minutes Jigson had worked on all six of them and could remove the hinges.

"Well done!" the twins congratulated. Abby hadn't forgotten to whistle down the tunnel every few minutes, and she only hoped she would be able to start heading back to the cavern shortly.

Jigson quickly slid his knife under the lid of the chest to loosen it, and then pulled at the lid. The twins held their breaths as the chest opened with a faint creak, revealing a navy, fabric bag resting at the bottom of it. Jigson lifted the heavy bag out with the utmost care and set it down on the floor of the tunnel.

Abby shone Lewis's torch in the chest to check that nothing was left inside while Andy, who was closest to the drawstring bag, opened it and shone his torch inside. Whether his eyes were shining of their own accord or whether the light was reflecting off the gold coins in the bag, Abby didn't know. Nor did she have the time to find out.

"I'm going back," she whispered hurriedly as she collected up the five nails with which to replace the hinges. "Goodbye."

"I'm coming too," Jigson answered. Turning to Andy, he breathed, "Stay here and protect that treasure. I'm going to follow your sister back to the cavern in case things don't go according to plan."

"In case Lewis Nickel doesn't keep his word?" Andy asked.

Jigson hesitated before nodding quickly in reply.

CHAPTER 19

Down, down, down the tunnel Abby crawled, whistling and calling frequently. Jigson helped her half-pull, half-carry the chest, filling it with any loose rocks and stones he could find.

Abby began chewing her lip as she realized that she had been away from the cavern for over fifteen minutes, and she hated to think what might have happened in her absence. *Lord,* she prayed fervently, *Lord, protect Father! Please, please protect us all!*

When they neared the tunnel entrance, Abby looked back and paused. Jigson put his finger to his lips and then closed the lid properly over the numerous rocks piled inside the chest. As Abby shone the torch backwards, he positioned the two hinges and quietly tapped the five nails back into place. The fact that one of the six nail-heads had sheared off was hardly noticeable. Then Jigson whispered, very softly, "If anything goes wrong, give a bird-call. God be with you."

Abby nodded slowly and then turned to complete the journey alone.

With a thumping heart, she dragged the heavy chest around the final bend in the tunnel. She knew that if it wasn't for adrenalin, she wouldn't have any strength in her state of mental, emotional, and physical exhaustion. The thought of facing Lewis Nickel and his thugs again threatened to drain the last drop of courage right out of her.

Lord, help me! she prayed as, with a final heave, she scraped the chest to the mouth of the tunnel and stopped there, panting, to look around the cavern. She closed her eyes in relief when she saw her father unharmed, seated on a rock, his head tilted forward in prayer. As she watched, he gazed up with eyes full of relief.

"So our little friend has returned," Lewis Nickel said with a sneering chuckle. "You know, if you had taken one minute longer, I would have called off our little arrangement."

"Sir," Abby replied, "that treasure chest weighs almost as much as I do."

A faint grin teased Lewis's features. "Rich, get her down from there," he commanded. "I want to see this treasure."

Rich roughly helped Abby off the ledge, and she stumbled forward onto her sore, chafed hands. Tears pricked hers eyes, but she blinked them back and rushed to her father's side.

"She's kept her side of the deal," Mr. Baker said in a deep voice. "Now let us go."

"No, no, no. Not so hasty!" Lewis laughed as Rich lowered the chest to the ground.

"That's a tiny chest," Rich said as he straightened up and stretched his back slowly. "Whatever is in there, it weighs quite a lot."

"Rocks!" Lewis replied. Abby's heart skipped a beat until Lewis's roar of laughter persuaded her that he had been making a joke, and she breathed again.

Lewis rubbed his hands together in expectation and then pulled out his revolver, aiming it at the lock. With a sinking feeling of dread, Abby became aware that he was about to open the chest. Without even realizing it, she grabbed tightly onto her father's arm.

"You can't open that chest!" she squeaked. "You can't do it!"

"And why not?" Lewis looked up with a half-hearted frown. "You don't want me to damage a historical artifact, hmm?" The men around him laughed.

"You can't open it!" Abby repeated desperately. "It doesn't belong to you!"

"You're quite right," Lewis nodded. "It belongs to my employer. But he won't mind me checking to see that everything is as it should be."

"No!" Abby replied. "It belongs to Mrs. Marge Jenkins, and you have no right to take it from her!" Then, as Lewis cocked his gun, she burst out with a cry of, "Cockle-doodle-doo!"

Mr. Baker looked at his daughter in surprise, and some of the men stared as if she had gone out of her mind. Just then a rock came hurtling out of the tunnel and hit Lewis squarely on the head. He slumped forward unconsciously, dropping his gun. It went off with a deafening bang that echoed around the cavern. The bullet ricocheted off the rock wall and zipped down the passage, thankfully harming no one. Lewis's startled accomplices drew their own guns just as another Lewis Nickel leapt bravely from the tunnel.

"Put down your guns, men!" Jigson roared. "As you see, I am Lewis Nickel, and this man, here," he said, pointing the toe of his boot at the unconscious figure, "is an imposter!"

The men glanced nervously at each other, their hands shaking in mid-air as they considered what course of action to pursue. Finally, one man looked at Jigson and called out, "Put your hands in the air! I am a police officer!"

Two other men repeated the statement and trained their guns on Jigson, and it was his turn to look stunned. In all the commotion, Rich grabbed the chest from under Lewis Nickel in a surprising display of strength, and he and the last remaining thug turned and fled down the rock passage.

Mr. Baker, thinking quickly, dashed forward to grab the gun the real Lewis had dropped, and then started in hot pursuit of Rich and his accomplice.

"Hand over your weapons!" one policeman commanded Jigson. "Turn around with your hands up high!"

"This is a terrible mistake!" Abby cried, jumping to her feet and rushing to the first policeman's side. "You need to catch those men! This man is not a real criminal, but those thugs who are escaping . . . are!"

"Then . . . who's the real Lewis Nickel?" the policeman stammered.

"That man!" Jigson answered, and Abby pointed to the unconscious figure.

"Please, please, sir!" Abby pleaded. "My father has gone after those two men, but there's no telling what could happen to him!"

"All right," the police officer nodded. "Frank and Harry, go after them. I can handle this."

The other two men turned and dashed down the tunnel, and their footsteps could be heard echoing back for a few minutes.

"So, why are there two Lewis Nickels?" the confused police officer asked.

Jigson quickly explained the basics of the situation, after which the police officer, sufficiently persuaded, put his gun back in its holster. He walked over to the unconscious Lewis Nickel and checked his wrist for a pulse before examining his head.

"Is he badly hurt?" Jigson asked, a hint of anxiety in his voice.

"I can't tell," the police officer replied. "He's got a strong pulse. I can't see anything on his head other than a nasty bump."

"Good," Jigson nodded. "I didn't intend anything more than to knock him unconscious."

The police officer looked up at him with an expression that Abby wasn't sure whether to identify as impressed, disapproving, or both.

"We need to get out of here," Jigson said, changing the subject. "I suggest we take the tunnel route," he said, waving his hand up at the hole in the cave wall.

"Can we take Mr. Nickel with us?"

"Certainly," Jigson nodded. "I'll help you."

The police officer seemed uncertain as to whether he really wanted Jigson's help or not. Either way, the three of them, plus the unconscious criminal, were soon heading down the tunnel for what Abby hoped was the last time that day. Abby led the way, Jigson came after, dragging Lewis Nickel behind him, and the police officer brought up the rear. He and Jigson took turns to pull the unconscious man along, as it was an exhausting task.

They finally came to the end of the tunnel, where they met a surprised Andrew Baker guarding the treasure.

"What's going on?" he asked nervously when he saw one Lewis Nickel crawling behind Abby, another Lewis Nickel who was limp, and an apparent thug bringing up the rear. Andy grabbed the fabric bag, preparing to fly out the hole if necessary.

"It's all right, Andy," Abby assured. "The real Lewis is unconscious, and this other man is a police officer in thug disguise."

"That sounds like quite a story," Andy said, raising his eyebrows. "I'd love to hear what happened back there. As for the treasure, what should I do with it? It's too heavy for me to carry."

Jigson and the policeman both agreed that the treasure should stay hidden in the tunnel, at least until the situation was safe enough to remove it.

They emerged into the open air, one by one. The twins watched as one Lewis Nickel came out the hole, pulling another Lewis Nickel behind him.

"Oh!" Andy suddenly said. "I wish I had my camera—that would make a great photo."

"Where is your camera?" Abby asked.

"I left it in the motorboat when I swam to warn you."

Once they were all out the tunnel, the policeman bent down to handcuff Lewis Nickel. Then he checked the limp criminal for weapons and found a long knife strapped around his shin, under his trouser-leg. He frowned and pointed to the empty gun-holster at the man's waist.

"My father took that gun when he started chasing the criminals who had taken the chest," Abby explained.

"I see," the policeman nodded, straightening up. "I need to find out what happened to those criminals who were getting away, but I can't leave Mr. Nickel."

"We'll look after him for you," Andy offered.

The policeman shook his head. "He's a wanted man, and I can't afford to take any risks of him escaping."

"Well then, we can be your eyes and ears," Andy volunteered. "We'll find out what's going on for you."

"I don't think your parents would want you kids to get involved," the policeman replied.

"Well, Sir, I can recommend the boy as an expert tree-climber," Jigson vouched. "He could be on look-out duty for you, and keep an eye out for approaching criminals."

Andy nodded eagerly, and dashed off to the trees to prove the evaluation.

"Tree-climber?" the policeman muttered in bewilderment. "Tree-climbing isn't allowed in some counties!"

"Oh, sir, these are extraordinary circumstances," Jigson replied. "Besides, that rule that might not even apply to this island."

The policeman shrugged. "All right, then. Just this once."

"Thank you," Jigson said. "Now, I really should be going to check on the rest of the members of this family. They were being held prisoners against their will, and I fear the situation could easily turn into one involving hostages."

"You're right," the policeman agreed.

"But Mr. Jigson, you're not armed," Abby pointed out.

"Unfortunately not. I'll just have to think of something."

Jigson turned and jogged away, slowing as he peered around the side of the hill. He crept forward silently. Then he was lost from view.

Jigson had just disappeared when there was the sound of a gunshot in the direction of the sea. The policeman's head turned quickly as he tried to determine the location of the sound. Then came another sharp report.

"The cliff!" Abby whispered. "The shots are coming from the bottom of the cliff!"

"Stay here," the policeman instructed sternly, and then began running towards the cliff edge. He stopped, dropped onto his belly, and inched his way forward the last bit of the way, peering cautiously down.

Down at the bottom of the cliff, gunshots were ringing out and bullets were whizzing back and forth. The policeman soon came to realize the cause of the fight.

The tide was coming back in, and the water was already knee-deep. The rock structure along the cliff was such that after exiting the cave, one could be sheltered from view until it became necessary to go around a rocky outcrop extending into the sea.

Rich, the other criminal, and the man guarding the boat inside the cave had almost reached the outcrop when Mr. Baker and the two policemen had exited the cave. Mr. Baker had fired one bullet, warning the criminals that they couldn't escape without the risk of being shot. A gunfight ensued, with the criminals trying to shoot their potential captors, and the policemen trying to stall the criminals long enough for the tide to prevent their escape to the beach.

The policeman watched from the cliff top for about a minute before taking aim at a rock near one of the criminals. He hoped to scare them into surrendering by letting them know they were being watched from above. He had cocked the gun when there was a sharp, reverberating report of a pistol from the other side of the cliff top, and stones came tumbling down the cliff wall beneath the policeman. His fingers reflexively responded to the surprise by pulling the trigger, causing the same dust and stone-shattering to occur on the other side of the cliff wall.

The men below looked up in consternation while the policeman looked up to see who had fired from the other side of the cliff top. The two men on the opposite sides of the cliff top caught sight of each other at just the same moment. They stared at each other in stunned silence for a second or two, and then the other man, Billy, leapt to his feet and ran back in the direction of the beach. The policeman took up the chase.

****

Jigson had just crept behind the hill when there was the sound of gunshots. He was about to turn back to see what was going on when he had an idea.

He sprinted forward, as fast as he could, and soon came into view of Martin and the Bakers. Martin stood up nervously, his hand on his gun holster as Jigson slowed to a stop and bent over, exaggerating his panting.

"Martin! Martin," he called between breaths. "The game is up! Some of my men were police in disguise, and as you can hear, there's a battle going on down there."

"So what do we do?" Martin asked uncertainly.

"We have to get away before more police arrive. And the only way we're going to get to a boat is by pretending that I'm the fake Lewis Nickel, and I've captured you."

"Are you sure that's a good idea?" Martin raised his eyebrows.

Jigson nodded angrily. "Of course it is!" he snapped. "Do you think I've come all this way to rescue *you*? Of course not! I can only escape by pretending to be the undercover agent in cahoots with the police. The only way I can do that is by pretending to arrest you. Now give me your gun!"

Martin hesitantly handed the gun over, which Jigson snatched from him. "Put your hands behind your back," Jigson snapped again. "You there," he said, nodding to Phil. "You're not tied up, are you? Then get me some rope!"

"Wh..what about the prisoners, Mr. Nickel?" Martin stammered, slightly intimidated by the bullying man.

"Oh, never mind them," Jigson replied as he hastily bound Martin's hands. "They're of no further use to us. Now stop calling me Mr. Nickel, understand? Do you understand?!"

"Yes!"

"Good. Now walk on," Jigson instructed, prodding Martin with the barrel of his gun. Then, in a slightly gentler voice, he said, "Prisoners, please follow me."

Mrs. Baker looked questioningly at Phil. "Is that . . . you-know-who?" she asked in a whisper.

"It must be," Phil answered. "A real criminal wouldn't expect us to follow him without being threatened or coerced."

"If you ask me," Alec grunted, "that's the fake Mr. Nickel. His voice is richer and less metallic than the other one."

Phil nodded in agreement.

They all stood up, rather stiff from their long period of inactivity, and began walking as fast as they could to catch up to the man prodding Martin along. After a few minutes, they all rounded a bend by a hill and there caught sight of Abby pacing restlessly on the grass beside a limp figure. Upon hearing a pigeon call, Phil looked up at the trees nearby and smiled when he spotted Andy waving.

When they got close to the limp figure, Martin was shocked to see Abby dash forward and address "Mr. Nickel" with, "Oh, thank the Lord! You've arrived just in time. There's a gunfight going on down, there and I haven't been able to see anything because the policeman told me to stay by Lewis Nickel."

"Where is the policeman?" Jigson asked.

"He was joining the gunfight from the cliff top when he spotted Billy doing the same thing. They both ran in the direction of the beach."

"The beach!" Jigson exclaimed.

"The boats!" Phil cried.

"The boats?" Martin repeated.

"Yes!" Jigson cried. "Billy is going to try to rescue his accomplices by boat; after all, the tide should be coming in."

"We have to help the policeman stop him!" Phil exclaimed.

"Yes," Jigson agreed. "Now, I suggest that everybody stays here and guards these crooks while I see what I can do to help the police. It's best that I take this gun with me. Phil, tie Martin up properly."

Martin had guessed by then that he'd been tricked, but there was nothing he could do about it. Phil bound the man's hands and feet securely while Jigson kept the gun handy.

When that was done, Jigson went to peer over the cliff edge and examine the situation. Nothing had changed, and he soon stood up and ran in the direction of the beach. The Bakers, meanwhile, found themselves in a role reversal with Martin.

In an hour, the action was all over. Jigson had found Billy and the policeman locked in a deadly tussle. Their guns had both run out of bullets, and the men had resorted to brute force. Jigson's arrival with a gun, therefore, ended the matter quickly. In minutes, he and the policeman had marched Billy back to where the Bakers were guarding the others. Lewis Nickel was just starting to come around, and Jigson decided to give the loaded gun to the policeman guarding the prisoners.

"My mission was to capture Lewis Nickel," the policeman said. "Therefore I must make sure he doesn't get away."

Jigson nodded in understanding. "Very well," he said, handing the loaded Glock 17 to the policeman. "May I swap this gun for yours?"

"Mine is out of bullets," the policeman said in surprise.

"That doesn't matter," Jigson replied. "It's just for show."

The policeman willingly handed over his empty gun. Then, just as Jigson was turning to leave, Phil asked, "Can I come with you?"

"You certainly can," Jigson nodded. "The more the merrier. But it would help if you also had a gun for show."

"There's one in Billy's holster," Abby said quickly.

Jigson nodded. "That one is empty too."

Phil bent over and took Billy's Beretta from its holster before following as Jigson led the way back to the beach in a sprint. They both jumped into the remaining functional motorboat. Though Phil had been resting for a long time, Jigson had been active all day and was understandably weary. Nevertheless, he took control of the boat and sped out of the bay towards the cave. He and Phil held their breaths as they rounded the outcrop of rock and found themselves entering the zone of gunfire.

To their surprise, they caught sight of Mr. Baker and two policemen in the motorboat they'd left inside the cave. They later learned that Mr. Baker had had the idea to pull it out the cave once the tide was high enough. With the boat, Mr. Baker and the policemen had a definite advantage over the criminals, who had to clamber up the rock face to avoid the powerful waves that smashed against the cliff.

"Those criminals are armed," Phil reminded Jigson quickly as the latter moved the boat closer to the rock face. "And we're not."

"I know," Jigson muttered. "Do as I do."

Once the boat was in position, Jigson turned and poised his gun menacingly at the men clinging desperately to the rock wall. Phil followed suit, trying to look confident despite the fact that his gun was useless.

"Surrender yourselves and come aboard, and we will show you mercy," Jigson's voice boomed over the pounding waves, "or be at the mercy of the tide! Make your choice!"

A few heart-thumping moments followed, with no response from the three criminals. The absence of gunshots made everything seem eerily silent.

Phil was sure that minutes were creeping slowly by as he stood in the swaying boat beside Jigson. They both stayed rooted in the same posture, their legs splayed for balance, their arms out straight in front of them, and their hands gripping the guns so hard that their knuckles turned white. Wind blew and ruffled their hair. Waves rolled by under the boat and then collided against the cliff, sending white spray into the air and spattering them with water droplets. Phil hoped his determined frown hid the fear that he felt certain showed in his eyes.

"Make your choice!" Jigson repeated in a steady voice. "We're not staying here forever!"

After a few more moments of suspense, one of the men jumped from his perch on the cliff, plunging into the foaming, chilly water and swimming strongly toward the boat. Phil and Jigson helped him aboard, Jigson taking his gun and handing it to Phil with a secretive nod. At last they were no longer defenseless.

"Sit here," ordered Jigson curtly, "and keep quiet." While Phil kept a watch on the captive, Jigson again addressed the men on the cliff. As he spoke, the other motorboat came up.

"Men, there is nowhere left for you to go on this island. Your accomplices, including Lewis Nickel, are captured. Surrender yourselves, and don't make this any harder than it needs to be," Jigson yelled.

"What will happen to the treasure?" Rich called down. The others were surprised to hear Jigson's reply.

"You can keep the contents of the chest if you come down now," Jigson answered.

"What?" Phil gaped in astonishment. Murmurs of shock and surprise came from the other motorboat.

"I know what I'm doing, Phil," Jigson said quietly.

"How do we know we can trust you?" Rich demanded.

"Upon my honor, I give my word," Jigson replied. "You may keep whatever's in the chest—but not the chest itself—if you come down."

"No, wait!" Mr. Baker cried. "I know you're trying to help, but the treasure isn't yours to give away."

Mr. Baker's outcry came too late, for the two criminals had already jumped off the rock wall and into the waves. They both swam to a cleft at the water level of the cliff, and there they waited for Jigson to bring the boat closer, which he did. The chest, which had been too heavy to carry up the cliff, had been securely wedged in the gap.

The two men handed over their guns, and then Phil and Jigson helped them aboard and heaved the chest onto the floor of the boat.

"You can't have been serious about your promise, Mr. Jigson. Please take it back!" Phil pleaded.

"He can't," Rich sneered. "He'd better not. He made a promise of honor— and he can't change that now."

Jigson simply said, "I intend to stand by my promise. You'll understand soon, Phil."

He turned the boat around, and Mr. Baker and the policemen followed as they sped toward the bay.

They landed, pulled the boats up the shore, and then marched their prisoners up the beach. Rich was made to carry the treasure chest, which he did with a grin.

One of Lewis's accomplices elbowed him and hissed, "You know you're going to end up in jail. How on earth do you think you're going to keep your grip on the treasure then, eh?"

By the time the criminals had been marched all the way to the hill, Rich was tiring under the weight of the chest. When he was allowed to sit down, he let out a deep sigh of relief and flopped on the grass.

Lewis Nickel, who was by then wide awake with no injury except a nasty headache, looked angrily around, his eyes demanding an explanation for why Rich had the chest. Rich taunted his foe with a sneering laugh.

"Why does he have the chest?" Lewis asked, incensed.

Mrs. Baker, relieved to see her husband, welcomed him back, her eyes questioningly searching his face for the cause of his sadness. "What is it, dear?"

"Jigson," Mr. Baker breathed, "Jigson promised Rich the treasure if he surrendered."

"Pardon?" Mrs. Baker asked, her eyes wide in surprise.

"What did you say?" Lewis Nickel demanded.

Jigson said, "I promised that Rich could keep the contents of the chest if he surrendered."

"Did you really?" Abby asked with an incredulous laugh.

Andy's face broke into a broad grin and he chuckled mischievously. "Has he seen the reward of his compliance yet?"

"No he hasn't," Jigson replied. "Rich, would you like to open the chest? I think you'll find that the hinges come off easier than you would expect."

Rich didn't need any further encouragement. He quickly began working at the nails holding the hinges in place, and as Jigson had predicted, they came out fairly easily. Rich pulled the chest lid open with a heave, and then drew back with an expression of surprise and dismay.

"Rocks?" he muttered, digging his hands inside the chest and throwing the rocks out in an attempt to find something valuable beneath them. "Rocks?! This chest is full of rocks?" He looked up in disbelief and fury. Meanwhile, Lewis had burst into uncontrollable laughter as he watched the proceedings.

"What...?" Mr. Baker stammered. "How did that happen?"

The twins looked at each other and beamed. "It was my idea," Andy said excitedly.

"Yes," Abby nodded. "Mr. Jigson helped us open the chest and fill it with rocks before I returned to the cavern. That's why I was so distressed when Mr. Nickel was about to open it."

Mr. and Mrs. Baker, Phil, and Alec laughed heartily when they understood what had happened. When the matter was explained to Rich, he became very sullen. "You cheated me," he growled fiercely.

Jigson shook his head. "I promised you the contents of the chest, and I didn't claim it was filled with treasure. As for the rocks, maybe you could take them along to prison if you wanted to."

CHAPTER 20

Abby sighed contentedly as she settled down on the couch in the holiday home. Her whole family had made it safely off the island—and that certainly was an answer to prayer.

The police had escorted the criminals safely to the Cornish shore, and Jigson oversaw the transportation of the treasure, by helicopter, back to Hertfordshire for safe-keeping. Alec returned to the harbor with extra money for the additional day he'd spent on the island, and with a good story to tell.

After the suspense and danger of the adventure, the Bakers were exhausted and grateful for the chance to catch their breaths. They were so convinced that they would be bored by hum-drum tourism, however, and so eager to get back to Hertfordshire and Old Marge, that they decided to leave the next day.

****

The Bakers arrived back in Hertfordshire after a very long but scenic journey. It felt shorter than it otherwise would have because the children took turns to read aloud from Lloyd's diary. The story was very interesting, especially the parts about fishing, fierce storms, and, finally, the accident with the falling tree.

Andy was reading when the car pulled up outside Grandfather Wilson and Granny Janet's cottage. He quickly finished the entry before slipping a bookmark into the old diary and getting out to help unpack the trunk.

"We're nearly finished the diary, aren't we?" Abby asked.

Andy nodded. "Just a page to go."

It was around four o'clock in the evening, and the sun was scattering golden rays over the cottage. The front door opened, and the grandparents came out to welcome the Bakers back.

"We were very excited when you told us over the phone that you'd found the treasure," Grandfather Wilson said. "I'd love to hear the whole story, but we should head to the Richards' house as soon as your luggage is inside."

"And perhaps once you've had a quick cup of tea," Granny Janet suggested.

"Are we going to the Richards' house?" Abby asked.

"Oh, yes," Mr. Baker nodded.

"I forgot to tell you that the Richards have invited us over for supper and to tell our adventure," Mrs. Baker said. "Marge is at their house."

"Great!" Abby exclaimed excitedly. "So I will get the chance to see Julie's horses after all."

The Bakers didn't have many bags to bring inside, and they were soon gratefully refreshing themselves with tea and home-baked cookies. Duke was madly excited to see the children again, and they were just as pleased to see him.

Andy was reaching for another choc-chip cookie when the doorbell rang.

Grandfather Wilson and Granny Janet looked at each other.

"Who could that be?" Granny Janet wondered aloud.

"I'm not sure," Grandfather Wilson replied.

He started to get up when Granny Janet said, "Don't worry dear, I'll get the door. You need to look after that foot of yours."

She left the room, and the others overheard her exchange a few words with a man before coming back into the living room. She was followed by a familiar figure—a lithe and agile gentleman with reddish-brown hair.

"Detective!" Phil beamed. "It's good to see you again."

Detective Mortimer smiled as he received similar greetings from the rest of the Bakers and shook their hands.

"I was tempted to head down to Cornwall, but you were already on your way back here."

"Well, Detective," Phil said, "I'm sure your side of the story is just as interesting as our own, and I'd love to hear it."

The detective stuck his hand inside his coat and pulled out a rolled-up newspaper. With a grin, he asked, "Excuse me, but are you the family that was in the paper today?"

He held out the newspaper, which Mr. Baker took with a surprised expression and opened for everybody to see. On the front cover was a picture of a family climbing out of a motorboat. Mrs. Baker, Abby, and Tom were on the dock. The headline blazed: "American Family Finds Cornish Treasure." Mr. Baker's eyes skimmed down the page.

"This must have been done by that news reporter we met at Alec's harbor," Mrs. Baker said.

"Yes," Mr. Baker nodded. "He got most of the story right."

Abby looked up at the detective. "Did you arrange this?"

"No," Detective Mortimer replied. "I didn't know anything about it until I happened to see these for sale. Naturally, I had to buy one."

"Well," Phil paused, "Alec was gone for two days when he was only expected to be gone for one. His assistant at the harbor would have been worried, and probably notified the police. The police must have known about the situation on the island because they'd already sent men to capture Lewis Nickel. Word must have leaked out to the news reporter somehow."

"Do you think the assistant was the one who rescued us, then, by sending the police?" Abby asked.

Phil shook his head slowly. "Those police were already in Lewis Nickel's confidence. Gaining his trust must have taken some time."

Detective Mortimer smiled. "A good observation, Phil, but not an entirely accurate one. Those men were in Lewis Nickel's confidence because they had been sent to help him by his employer."

"His employer?" Abby frowned.

"Of course!" Phil gasped. "I've been meaning to ask you, Detective, if you know who the kingpin is? It can't have been Lewis Nickel."

Detective Mortimer nodded slowly and discreetly. "Lewis Nickel was just an employee. His employer is safely behind bars."

"Were the policemen who came with Mr. Nickel undercover agents, like Mr. Jigson?" Andy asked.

"They must have been, mustn't they?" Abby joined. "How would they otherwise have gotten so deep into the employer's confidence that he would send them to help Mr. Nickel?"

"No, they weren't agents like Jigson," the detective replied. "Let me explain. By the time you arrived on the island, we had already arrested the kingpin of this operation. Because Rich and his accomplices were undoubtedly going to catch you, we had to be very careful about how we handled things. We didn't want you to become hostages with your lives threatened, so instead of sending hordes of police to rescue you, we made the kingpin tell Mr. Nickel to postpone his trip one day so that he could be joined by three extra men. Those extra men were the police, but he had no idea of that.

"Moreover," the detective continued, "postponing Mr. Nickel's arrival meant that we could send Jigson to pose as Mr. Nickel and make sure you were all right. From what I heard, he even succeeded in freeing you for a while."

"Yes," Mr. Baker nodded.

"That's what enabled us to find the treasure before the real Lewis Nickel did," Phil added.

"So if the real Lewis Nickel wasn't the kingpin, who was?" Mr. Baker asked. "Can you tell us, detective?"

The detective nodded again. "His name is Mr. Hamlyn Toole. He's the trustee of Bracken Estate."

There were gasps of surprise and incredulity around the room.

"I thought Mr. Richards was the owner of Bracken Estate," Andy said with a frown.

The detective shook his head. "Mr. Richards is only the manager. He looks after the estate on Mr. Toole's behalf."

Abby had a confused expression on her face. "Don't the Brackens own Bracken Estate?"

Detective Mortimer nodded. "Mr. Toole was charged by the court to look after the Estate until Cyril Bracken is old enough to inherit it."

"Why would Mr. Toole be so desperate to get his hands on the Jenkins treasure?" Mrs. Baker asked.

"Simply put, the answer is debt," the detective replied. "Mr. Toole was a gambler who fell into debt and needed a large sum to save himself. The easiest way to do that, he reasoned, was to find the legendary treasure whose map had been locked away for years within the walls of Bracken Hall.

"He himself stayed beneath the radar, trying to evade notice from his creditors and Mr. Richards. His thugs broke into Bracken Hall and successfully stole the treasure map. Then they stole Edward Jenkins's diaries so that nobody would ever know whether the tale was legend or not. The only thing he didn't take into account was Old Marge Jenkins's memory. The fact that you took her so seriously proved to be his undoing."

"Coupled with your excellent brain and calculating detective work," Phil added.

"It sounds like Mr. Toole needed to learn the lesson of the Jenkins brothers," Abby said. "Laziness and greed brought nothing but misery to their lives."

The others nodded in agreement.

Mrs. Baker glanced at her watch. "We agreed to arrive at the Richards' house at five thirty. That leaves us only a few minutes before we have to depart."

The Bakers drove to Bracken Estate once more, bringing Detective Mortimer in their car, since he had also been invited for supper. Instead of turning towards the Hall, they continued driving straight for a few minutes. Then they turned down a little side road, and drove through an area scattered with trees. They came to a gate marked 'Private—No Public Access,' and the grandparents, who were leading the way, pushed the button for the intercom. At that, the gate swung open, and they all drove through.

They entered a grassy clearing where a smart, red-brick house stood in the distance. The cars pulled up outside the house, and the Bakers admired the eye-pleasing selection of flowers sprouting from flower-pots against the wall.

The front door opened, and Mr. Richards ushered the guests inside the house. It was spacious and neat, but old photos on the walls added a touch of down-to-earth homeliness.

"Julie!" Mr. Richards called from the foot of the stairs before leading the way to the sitting room. Mrs. Richards had apparently been busy in the kitchen because she appeared with a dishtowel over her shoulder. Old Marge was seated in a wheelchair in the sitting room. Julie joined the group, and when she greeted Abby, she said, "Maybe after you've told us your adventure I can take you out to see the horses."

"Sounds great," Abby beamed.

They sat down and got comfortable, and then Mr. Richards plunged into conversation.

"We saw you in the newspaper this morning," he said. "Is the article accurate?"

"Mostly," Mr. Baker nodded. "We hired a skipper named Alec Gimsby to take us out to the island on Thursday morning, and we found the skeleton and diary of Lloyd, Edward Jenkins's son. We'd only read the beginning of his diary when three men arrived and held us hostage. When they realized they couldn't figure out the clues to the treasure themselves, they forced us to help them. We gave false leads wherever we could until they were ready to harm us in their exasperation. Thankfully, that's when an undercover agent arrived in the disguise of Lewis Nickel. We didn't realize it was him until he doped the three criminals that night and freed us. We had a few hours to find the treasure before the real Lewis Nickel arrived. Philip, Andrew, and Mr. Jigson went looking for the treasure in a cave, but the rest of us were captured."

Mr. Baker went on to describe the rest of what happened on the island. The Richards were very surprised at the danger and unpredictability of the series of events.

After the Richards had asked questions, Mr. Baker said, "We only know our side of the story, and would love to hear what happened on this end of it."

"Detective Mortimer is the best person to tell you that," Mr. Richards replied.

"Well," the detective began, "once I had investigated the two robberies at Bracken Hall, I suspected they were an inside job. They were too well executed to be otherwise. Secondly, I have learned over the years not to dismiss an idea simply because it seems far-fetched. Even though the treasure tale was unlikely to be true, I could think of no other reason why the map and diaries had been stolen.

"I reasoned that if the diaries were stolen to cover up any evidence, then Marge's accounts were of utmost importance. I listened to the recordings you made at the hospital, Phil, a number of times.

"Armed with that information, I began my research. I started at the logical starting place. If the robberies were an inside job, who better to arrange them than Mr. Toole himself? That led me on a track to discovering who he is, what his hobbies are, and finally, how deeply he is in debt. At that stage I knew I had discovered a suspect. Mr. Toole was a man with a motive.

"After that, things began to fall into place. Mr. Toole was lying low, and it seemed reasonable to believe that he would have hired men to do his work for him. That was when I sent Phil the message to look out, and to beware of men after the treasure. The more I investigated, the more evidence I found to prove my theory. I found out the names and details of the three men Mr. Toole had hired, commonly referred to as Rich, Billy, and Martin.

"By the time Phil asked if the men had found the treasure, I was deep enough in the investigation to know that Mr. Toole was becoming frustrated at their lack of results. Clearly they had not found it yet."

Phil nodded. "The next message you sent was about the thugs having the map. How did you find that out?"

"The map had been stolen from Bracken Hall. When I found the original in Mr. Toole's possession, I needed no further evidence. He had obviously given his hired men a copy of it. With the stolen map were an old key, Edward's missing diaries, and a few other documents belonging to him. One of the documents mentioned a set of coordinates. When I discovered that they indicated an island off the Cornish coast, I sent them to you as a possible lead.

"We caught Mr. Toole the very next day, once you had left for the island, and we found out that he was sending Lewis Nickel there at midday if the hired men hadn't found the treasure by then. Mr. Toole's capture meant we could change his plans. We instructed him to delay Mr. Nickel, and we sent three policemen to join him."

"I see," Mr. Baker said. "It's amazing how things slotted into place at just the right moments. If this journey hadn't been carefully orchestrated by the Lord, it would have ended very differently."

Mrs. Baker nodded. "He not only orchestrated things in our lives, though. He planned everything even in Edward Jenkins's life."

"You're right, and I had just been pondering the same thing," Mr. Baker said. "If Edward's ship hadn't been wrecked, the treasure wouldn't have been lost. If Edward hadn't been wounded in battle and captured by pirates, he would have retrieved the chest himself."

"If Lloyd hadn't gone out to search for the chest, it would have stayed off the coast of Lizard, and the thugs would have found it before us," Phil added.

Abby nodded. "If Lloyd hadn't gone searching on the particular day that he did, he wouldn't have been caught in a storm and stranded on the island."

"Yes," Andy agreed, "and if it hadn't rained, he would have died of dehydration."

"Exactly!" Mr. Baker agreed. "And just think about the treasure—if Lloyd hadn't coded the clues he made, we couldn't have misled the thugs."

"They would have found it quickly, and stranded or harmed us," Mrs. Baker said.

"Isn't it amazing to see how God works everything out, all the way through history?" Phil thought aloud.

The rest of the evening passed very pleasantly. Mrs. Richards had made fish, chips, and mushy peas as a truly British meal for the American family to enjoy. For dessert, she'd made Bramley apple crumble. Julie then showed the Baker children around the stables, and there was even time for a short ride along a bridleway on the estate.

The next day the treasure was handed over to Marge Jenkins in a great ceremony held at Bracken Hall. First, Edward Jenkins' diaries were restored to the library. Then the Bakers had the chance to tell their story to the locals and journalists attending. Mr. Baker was careful to explain the Biblical reason they had set out to search for the treasure in the first place.

Once Mr. Baker was finished, Peter Richards stood up and said, "My wife Sue and I were greatly impacted by the Bakers' motivation in helping my mother-in-law, especially when considering all the dangers they were exposed to. All the time they were in Cornwall, we were pondering the meaning of their desire to help widows. Now, I think, we are both ready to admit the selfishness of our way of thinking, and we will do everything we can to ensure that Mrs. Fielding stays in her own cottage as long as her health allows. I want to extend a personal thanks to the Bakers for helping us come to this view."

The Bakers were understandably pleased and touched to hear this account.

Then Phil and Andy carried forward the chest, veiled in a sheet of red velvet. They set it on a small table beside Old Marge, and then Abby drew back the velvet. Mr. Baker handed the elderly lady an old key, which she slid into the lock on the chest. The audience held their breaths as the lock sprung open. Marge pulled back the latch of the chest, and then carefully lifted the lid. Slowly, she opened the navy blue, drawstring bag, and a gasp of astonishment went up from the crowd when she drew out a handful of gold coins.

Sue Richards bent over and whispered something into her mother's ear, at which Old Marge beckoned for the Bakers to come closer.

Sue seemed to be trying to dictate something for her mother to repeat, but the elderly lady shook her head. She looked Mr. Baker in the eye, and all she said was, "Thank you."

Mr. Baker stared in surprise at the gold coin extended to him by that frail, well-aged hand, and he did not move for a few moments.

"Thank you," Old Marge repeated, as if that was explanation enough.

Mr. Baker reached one hand forward tentatively, at which Old Marge grasped it and pushed the gold coin into his palm.

Then, before Mr. Baker could say anything, she motioned for Mrs. Baker to step forward, holding out one gold coin as she had before.

"Oh Marge," Mrs. Baker muttered, her eyes misting up at the elderly lady's generosity. "You are too kind."

"Thank you," Old Marge said by way of reply.

The Baker children, Tom included, were rewarded in the same way as their parents, each receiving one gold coin.

Finally, Mr. Baker reached into his suit pocket and pulled out a leather-bound book, worn with age. He held it out to Marge.

"This is a treasure in itself," he said. "It is the diary of Lloyd Jenkins, the son of Edward Jenkins. The history within its pages is remarkable and a true blessing to read."

Old Marge took it gratefully, running her fingers over the old leather.

"The famous diary," Sue said, excitement in her voice. "Thanks for finding and bringing it back."

Mr. Richards nodded. "I'm sure it's priceless family history. I am very eager to read it; perhaps we can go through it as a family."

The Bakers left England the very next evening. The farewells at the airport to Grandfather Wilson, Granny Janet, and Old Marge were particularly emotional ones, and not one Baker disappeared into customs with a dry eye.

When they got home to their beloved farm, they were full of mixed emotions—excitement at being home, gratitude for safety and the memories they had, and melancholy that their English adventure was at an end.

That afternoon, Mr. Baker announced that he had received an e-mail from Peter Richards. Everybody was drawn, as if magnetically, to hear what Mr. Richards had to say.

"How considerate," Mr. Baker said. "Mr. Richards writes, 'I want to thank you and your family, once again, for the huge part you played in restoring the Jenkins treasure. The gold was only a part of it, as we have recently discovered. You may not have heard that the document Detective Mortimer discovered with the coordinates on it was a title deed. Since the coordinates pinpoint the exact location of Lloyd's Island, my mother-in-law is now the confirmed heir to it!'"

Mr. Baker paused as there were gasps of surprise from the listeners.

"Lloyd was stranded on an island his father owned? That's unbelievable!" Phil exclaimed.

"Now that *can't* be coincidence," Abby said.

"It can only be Providence!" Mr. Baker said in awe.

Mrs. Baker nodded. "If I remember correctly, Lloyd didn't seem to have any idea that the island was his father's."

Mr. Baker looked back at his screen to continue reading. "'With my mother-in-law's full agreement, Sue and I are going to open the island to the public and set up a museum there so that Lloyd Jenkins and his adventurous life will never be forgotten. Furthermore, we have decided to name the place Providence Island, as he would have wanted.'"

"Wow," Mrs. Baker muttered, touched, as Mr. Baker paused in his reading.

"'When we began reading Lloyd's diary last night, we noticed that there was a bookmark at the end of it. It must belong to you, and as you are probably in suspense to know the end of the story, I have scanned the last page and attached it below. Trusting that you had a pleasant journey home. Sincerely, Peter,'" Mr. Baker finished.

"That was thoughtful," Abby said. "I'd been thinking that we'll never know what happened to Lloyd. Did he die of his wounds when that tree fell on him, or did he pull through?"

Mr. Baker cleared his throat. "Let's find out. The entry is December 31, 1739. Just think—that's four months after he was stranded."

The others nodded. "And the last day of the year 1739," Abby added.

"It's amazing to think that we've had a glimpse of his life on the island," Mrs. Baker said.

"It certainly is," Mr. Baker agreed. "Well this is his last entry, just two days after the accident. 'My body is battered and bruised, especially my arm, which is swollen and bloodstained. I spent the night in fitful dozing punctuated by the heated throbbing in my left arm, which I endeavoured to alleviate with cool water. I fear the wound is infected. If there was a doctor here, he might amputate the arm and so save me, but performing such an operation myself would mean certain death.

'The end of my life is nigh. The pain is so great that I see the sweet slumber of death as an ushering into eternal rest and fellowship with Christ. I do not fear passing into the next life, for the Lord has removed death of its sting and the grave of its victory.

'Strength leaves me. I must soon put down my pen, for writing is becoming more and more wearisome. O come, Lord, and bring me into life everlasting!'"

Mr. Baker's eyes traveled down the page to a final paragraph, written in barely legible scrawl, and in a choked voice he read, " 'I have in these final moments struck upon a name for this island which the Lord has seen fit to have me call my own these weeks. I believe the name fits the place well, and in the unlikely event that anyone should find this diary, I hope the name will remain. Here, with the strength of my last breaths, I christen this place "Providence Island," for the Lord has here revealed to me the glorious mercy and goodness of His Providence for His children. To Him alone be the glory forever. Amen.'"

The End

SCRIPTURE REFERENCES USED FOR THE RIDDLES

1 Kings 17:3-4, "Get thee hence, and turn thee eastward, and hide thyself by the brook Cherith, that *is* before Jordan. And it shall be, *that* thou shalt drink of the brook; and I have commanded the ravens to feed thee there."

Rev. 20:10, "And the devil that deceived them was cast into the lake of fire and brimstone, where the beast and the false prophet *are,* and shall be tormented day and night for ever and ever."

Psalm 121:1-2, "I will lift up mine eyes unto the hills, from whence cometh my help. My help *cometh* from the LORD, Who made heaven and earth."

Matt. 8:23-26, "And when he was entered into a ship, his disciples followed him. And, behold, there arose a great tempest in the sea, insomuch that the ship was covered with the waves: but he was asleep. And his disciples came to *him,* and awoke him, saying, Lord, save us: we perish. And he saith unto them, Why are ye fearful, O ye of little faith? Then he arose, and rebuked the winds and the sea; and there was a great calm."

1 Sam. 22:1-2, "David therefore departed thence, and escaped to the cave Adullam: and when his brethren and all his father's house heard *it,* they went down thither to him. And every one *that was* in distress, and every one that *was* in debt, and every one *that was* discontented, gathered themselves unto him; and he became a captain over them: and there were with him about four hundred men."

John 1:42, "And he brought him to Jesus. And when Jesus beheld him, he said, Thou art Simon the son of Jona: thou shalt be called Cephas, which is by interpretation, A stone."

Other Scripture verses used for the story:

Rom 8:28, "And we know that all things work together for good to them that love God, to them who are the called according to *his* purpose."

Gal 6:9, "And let us not be weary in well doing: for in due season we shall reap, if we faint not."

Rom. 12:20- 21, "Therefore if thine enemy hunger, feed him; if he thirst, give him drink: for in so doing thou shalt heap coals of fire on his head. Be not overcome of evil, but overcome evil with good."

2 Cor. 12:9, "And he said unto me, My grace is sufficient for thee: for my strength is made perfect in weakness. Most gladly therefore will I rather glory in my infirmities, that the power of Christ may rest upon me."

1 Cor. 15:55, "O death, where *is* thy sting? O grave, where *is* thy victory?"

Rom. 6:23, "For the wages of sin is death, but the gift of God is eternal life in Jesus Christ our Lord."

"Learn to do well;

Seek judgment,

Relieve the oppressed,

Judge the fatherless,

Plead for the widow."

Isaiah 1:17 [emphases added]